Tom Hellberg

CLUBTOWN CROSSROADS

Limited Special Edition. No. 19 of 25 Paperbacks

The author is a retired architectural draughtsman who has also worked as an advertising manager in *Mind, Body, Spirit* magazine. He has been involved in highlighting the need for action on climate change and a former member of the Eco Worriers, an environmentally concerned band.

To all the characters I have met over the years.

Tom Hellberg

CLUBTOWN CROSSROADS

AUSTIN MACAULEY PUBLISHERS™

LONDON • CAMBRIDGE • NEW YORK • SHARJAH

A CIP catalogue record for this title is available from the British Library.

ISBN 9781528929707 (Paperback)
ISBN 9781528930628 (ePub e-book)

www.austinmacauley.com

First Published (2020)
Austin Macauley Publishers Ltd
25 Canada Square
Canary Wharf
London
E14 5LQ

Chapter 1

(7000l~5)

Clive was traipsing down the leafy street back from the town centre. It had been a difficult week in Frackburgh. Preoccupied with his own thoughts he glanced around over the street. At that moment, an ex-army jeep drove by, its three-whip antennas waving in the spring wind on its khaki body. He recognised it straightaway. It belonged to Pablo Perez, the one and only club owner in town. He was on his way back to his base.

He had been there last Saturday night with Beth. The Omegaplex was Pablo's pride and joy. It was also a source of some amusement and not a little concern in the small town. Beth had said that it reminded her of a working men's club, which had been taken over by a yuppie.

The date had not, regrettably, gone to plan. They had gone to see a local group, the Boo Rey Kendrick, a new romantic revival band, who lived and believed that they were Frackburgh's answer to Boy George and Jonathon Richmond. It had started well until the subject of Judd had come up.

Judd was his elder stepbrother. The son his father, Roy, never wanted him to meet; the quarrelsome brother who had bullied him ever since they had crossed paths. The brother who had come back to Frackburgh for god knows what reason.

'Wheeler dealer used-car man, perhaps?'

Beth had reminded him that she was an orphan who had been brought up by Catholic nuns. Not a pleasant memory obviously.

Dad's first marriage had hit the rocks and Judd had blamed him. His stepbrother had never accepted his new mother, Greta, and particularly a young nine-year-old Clive. It had been when he was four that his dad met Greta, far away in Scarborough. He had been too young to understand the divorce but he had felt the pain. Greta had her own daughter, a teenager called Louise, from a previous relationship. Whereas he had found this new step-mum loving and missed his own mother, Judd was a moody thirteen-year-old, who was always pushing the boundaries.

Four years later and after many crossed words, his brother had suddenly appeared, out of nowhere, back in his town. His dad, Roy, and especially his step-mum, Greta, were mystified as well. Now, his dad was disabled, it had certainly not been out of compassion – a quality he did not understand. Beth, who often worked behind the bar, seemed to know him well. That upset him even more, as he had the hots for her.

When he had started school, it was right here in Frackburgh, he had put down roots for life and gone on to study at the Fraisier Academy. He had even picked up the ancient sport of curling at the ice rink in Edinburgh. Now, this unwelcome harbinger from the dark past threatened to engulf him. It jarred with his newfound romance. He had only recently been going to watch bands and he was excited by the music he heard. His guitar playing had improved as he watched the other musicians.

Next weekend, they were due to see a real Jamaican dancehall band, Yellowman, inspiration to none other than Bob Marley himself. Yellowman (for there were five of them) were apparently on their way over the border to England to tour and would be doing their warm-up gig right here. This really was a coup for the town. Beth had told him last week that more ska bands were on the way from overseas and she would be on the bar.

'Mind you,' she said, 'I am not in favour of all these foreigners coming into town for all this adulation.'

He remembered those words; he hated racism.

He could not begin to imagine how Pablo had pulled the Omegaplex off, but they were flying into Edinburgh airport from Kingston, perhaps it was some budget airline deal. Their first English gig was here, in Frackburgh, of all places. The town's castle was on the tourist circuit and a network of bed and breakfasts thrived in the summer months.

So on that day, he was not in the best of moods, he might as well turn around and go back to the club which seemed to him, in this town, to be at the route of all things good and bad, so he turned on his heel and crossed the road.

Town of Frackburgh

CLIVE → tows ← PABLO PEREZ
(club owner)
LBETG:
Candia
OMEGAPLEX
SUSS
(older stepbrother)

SKA BAND

Sar CLUB

LOTS OF EXPLOSION,
LITTLE NARRATIVE.

Fam
(asriold) not GREEN (sister) Louise

(TELLS Not SHOWS)

Chapter 2

(450)

He strolled into the bar of the Omegaplex. At this time in the afternoon, it was virtually empty. Pablo himself was cleaning glasses behind the bar. Dire Straits was playing on the jukebox.

'Hello, son, back for some more music?' he quipped.

'I'll settle for a beer.' He looked around – the venue had been converted from a working men's club, Beth was right about that. The music was performed downstairs, the bar up here. It had a marble bar top, a laminate backset, optics in some hammered metallic pattern with mirrors and video screens. It would not have looked out of place in a central London sports bar, but it was upmarket for Frackburgh. How had Pablo done it? Yes, it filled up at weekends that was true, but on the weekdays, well, there were only five people here now.

In the corner, a young couple were deep in conversation. At the bar, a downbeat guy stared down at his almost empty glass. It looked like life was his personal problem. Another guy was on his computer, doing something to the satellite TV box.

'I'm looking forward to Yellowman,' Clive said.

'You can see on our Facebook page,' volunteered Pablo. 'I'm live streaming him, so he will be there for posterity.'

'How did you get the copyright for that?' Clive asked.

'I don't bother with that, he is only performing in Frackburgh after all.'

'Oh that's fantastic, Pablo,' replied Clive and thought to himself, *one day I will organise something here myself.*

'I'm finding my guitar playing is really coming on by listening to these bands,' Clive said. 'I feel at home in this place. Thank you, Pablo.'

They exchanged a smile.

Chapter 3

(558)

Judd was in no mood to answer the door. He was pretty sure Anya was his visitor, judging by the "rap rap" of her knuckles on the door and the barking of her hound, Igor the husky. It was early evening and he had just made tea. Anya was a Russian yuppie, who had come up from London the year before. She was a very needy woman about five years older than Judd.

He looked through the window – yes, it was Anya all right. There was a steely coldness in those blue Russian eyes. Had she come from the bookies? He cracked open the door and greeted her with little enthusiasm. 'You should have rung me first, I'm just sitting down to eat.'

'Comrade, I do apologise. I will take a glass with you.'

Judd responded, 'You better come in.'

Igor the husky followed and settled, paws forward on the carpet. The humans sat down. The bedsit was tiny, a little dingy, and pretty untidy. Anya took the sofa, stretching out her long legs. Judd sat down at his two-seater table and tucked into his stew.

'You haven't been gambling again, have you?' Anya was notorious for a flutter but generally seemed to lose more than she ever won. Anya scowled.

'What brings you here?' Judd added, 'You can have a vodka, though.'

Anya considered the offer and nodded and responded, 'I have a business proposition for you.'

Judd stopped mid-mouthful and thought, *now what?*

'I thought you would be interested in a partnership, comrade Judd. We could both benefit from Russian sources of funding I have in London. You could be living in style,

12

Judd,' she said, looking around the four cheerless walls, which barely seemed to exist. It was difficult to believe that anyone actually lived in this flat. It had two rooms in all, sparsely furnished with a limp sofa and a few chairs. She accepted Judd's proffered glass and sipped the searing liquid.

'Judd,' she said, 'how long have you been dealing? You are a dealer, aren't you?'

Judd looked her in the eyes. 'None of your business, is it, Anya?'

Anya re-joined, 'But, comrade, it could be.'

'Why would I want to be in business with you?'

Anya looked up. 'Because we could grow this business in a style you could only dream of, Judd.'

Judd had a quick think. It had been a strange dialogue. This was a hustle. He had been getting his supplies through the reggae bands that came to town and with the connivance of Pablo at the Omegaplex. He didn't really have a funding problem because he paid off the ganja to the bands with the mark-up he made on the deals, with a split for Pablo. It was much more lucrative than car trading.

He had hoped Anya had not worked that out. Clearly, Anya could expose him and ruin the whole business. He was curt. 'I need time to think about that, Anya. Now if you don't mind, I need to get out and about.'

He took his plate over to the sink and thought, *please, leave it, Anya*. He decided not to mention all this to Pablo for now.

'Don't leave it long, ring me, Judd.' With that, Anya turned and went straight out the door, followed out by her faithful hound. Igor sure was a beautiful husky and Anya was a sphinx.

Not somebody to be trusted, Judd thought.

Chapter 4

(500)

Ramos and Juliana were playing hide and seek. They had moved upstairs above the club when their mum had walked out on Pablo. Denise took a dim view of the whole Omegaplex project, she had wanted a family man, regular hours. Why couldn't Pablo have stayed in his factory job?

Denise was a nurse at Frackburgh General, the newish town hospital, and there was an uneasy truce with Pablo over their care. At nine and seven-year-olds, they were inseparable. She was aware that she had to put them first or she would not be able to afford to look after them on the salary of a nurse. As an architect, Pablo had enlisted Clive's help to re-model the flat above the club.

'What's for tea?' Ramos asked Pablo.

'What time is Mum picking us up, Dad?' interjected Juliana.

'You know that guys!' Pablo re-joined.

He squirmed inwardly, as Juliana stomped out of the lounge and Ramos stared blankly at it him, then followed. A choice between family ties and his burning ambition for the Omegaplex was tearing him apart. He slammed the door and trundled down the stairs to the bar. He needed to open up for the evening. Tomorrow night would be the busiest since he opened. He considered a swift half but put it out of his mind.

He would always need more punters, like Clive, for example. That's why he had his own website and Facebook page. Had he not said that he might host an open mike night? Clive was already drawing up plans for the flat-to-be for Pablo. Clive was often out of money by the end of the month and Pablo would sub him a few beers. Perhaps then he would give some of his time to help at the club, like Beth, who he seemed to fancy.

He chuckled. It was great to own his own club and this Saturday was the biggest gig so far. Snatches of memory came back to him. Fearful memories came back to him. He remembered those long working days in his previous existence. The dreary shifts he had at Kinnock Magnetics, the hard disc manufacturing plant set on the grimy, decaying industrial estate. Foul chemicals, long shifts, Good riddance! He had come a long way from Portugal, all those years ago. He put on his grey felt hat, gave it a tap and closed the door behind him.

Chapter 5

(250)

Clive heard his mobile vibrate and picked it up. 'Yes?'

'It's Dad here, son.' Roy always checked up on him every evening about this time, an irritation which had started since he left Scarborough. It did seem pretty pointless now that they both lived in the same town; well-intentioned as it might be. He didn't blame him. This insecurity was more to do with his stepbrother Judd, he was sure.

He was correct. 'When did you last see Judd, Clive?' he quizzed.

'Why? What has he been up to now?'

'I hear things about him, just gossip; from the supermarket office actually.' There was an audible sigh. 'Nothing definite.' Roy was referring to the Muirside, a council estate on the barren east side of town, a sink estate of serious hardcore drug users and life losers. It was located next to a barren moorland bog. People living together in the poorest housing, on the front line and destined to be locked up.

'I see.' Why did he have to find himself dogged by this malingerer, not really a fellow sibling, who seemed to have a grudge match with the whole of the world? 'So what, what do I care?'

'What can I do? He is an adult now.'

All this on a Friday night after a long week at the office. 'Leave it, Dad.' He rung off.

Only last weekend, he had an extended conversation with Beth, who seemed to be about her unfortunate Catholic orphanage upbringing. Her time there had left a serious dent in her psyche, he thought. Now there was something he did care about.

? LINK .

Chapter 6

(2007)

Beth was getting ready for her Saturday evening shift at the club. Her daughter Marilyn was lodged with a babysitter. Her baby was teething at the moment and she hadn't had a great deal of sleep to be sure. She pinned back her hair and set out the door. It was fortunate that Pablo's wife, Denise, had once again stepped in as she was not on shift at the hospital and had offered to look after the baby overnight, who would no doubt be fussed over by Ramos and Juliana, her children. She was an easy woman to trust, after her upbringing, a nurse herself. Her heart lurched, she was pretty certain Clive would be there. Had they arranged to meet? She couldn't remember what she said after he had stormed out. She had taken a fancy to him, but when he started on about his family, it was a big turn off, and her upbringing had not helped either.

She closed the door behind her and bounded out into the night. Well, whatever happened, she would do her job behind the bar with Monica as back-up and he would be on the other side of it. She would not be able to watch the famous dancehall artist but she would certainly hear him, as the sound would be blasting up from the basement stage. He was an albino genius, the one and only Yellowman. It would definitely be a busy night, the busiest ever.

Chapter 7

), 100.

It was filling up. It had just turned 9 pm. She looked around, no sign of Clive yet, but the band was not due on stage until 10 pm. The din in the bar was overwhelming and she and Monica were working hard. Pablo was somewhere downstairs changing a barrel. Would he be on the door tonight? Would they go over the fire limit for the basement? They took the money down the hallway of the stairs. There had once been a snooker table down here. Pablo had cut off the legs at half height to make a stage, topping it off in chipboard. Over the last few weeks, it had been extended again to accommodate the size of the five-piece, this time using some old pallets and more chipboard and all painted with matt black emulsion. Pablo had set up his bar camera to record the stage area.

The soundcheck had been going on all afternoon or so it seemed to Pablo. The tour bus was parked down a side street, and the stage was occupied by two banks of keyboards, a drum kit, amplifiers, monitors and a lighting rig. The band was out taking a break before the main event. The sweet smell of cannabis drifted in from the outside. The bar didn't actually have a stage door, so all this had been lugged down the stairs well beforehand. Pablo was exhausted. Unless a lot of locals turned up, he would lose money. He was already down on advance ticket sales and not far short on the fire limit. That was a risk.

He would do well on the bar of course, which was now filling up. At best he would break even – except for Judd, the saving grace of the operation. Judd was ingratiating himself with the band. Pablo had made it crystal clear that there would be no dealing on the premises but his half share of the proceeds was making all the difference.

True, in the past he had been over-lenient with underage drinkers but he would not risk his licence again, not after the police raid a fortnight ago – when they came in to check. Luckily for him, there were no teenagers in that night, but it had been a wake-up call for sure. He had stressed to Beth and Monica that they must check all ID tonight and every night from now on. He had received 350 likes on the club's Facebook page, but the fire limit was the problem, he would have to turn away everyone when he reached 120.

His problem was that few of the Frackburgh clan had made the musical connection with Bob Marley. The Edinburgh crowd knew, though. They made up most of his pre-sales, about fifty out of the eighty sold so far. After all, it was their only Scottish gig.

Yellowman had been, in the 1960s, the dancehall prequel to the whole reggae revival; Bob Marley Island records, Coventry ska and even an Italian copycat had followed a generation later. He loved that music, indeed he was booking new cover bands all the time, but he needed to build up his town fan base. The town was small but there was a wide rural hinterland to tap. It was not a wealthy part of the world.

It was onwards and upwards. He finished connecting the barrel and returned upstairs. He reached the bar and shouted over to Beth, 'Guinness back on!' He winked. Then he came over as she started to pull the dark liquid. 'Could you help us out on the door tonight, hun?' She looked surprised. 'I need to stick with the band tonight,' he said. 'Look, I will start you off with the count, but when we reach the one-twenty limit, I need you to turn them away. Stay at the top door and be firm.'

'OK,' she replied cautiously. It would mean that when Clive came in, she would have to talk to him. 'Half an hour, OK?'

Just then, Clive walked in, with a woman she did not recognise, in tow. Thank goodness she was still behind the bar. She stared but forced an awkward smile and waited for their order.

'I was passing the bus station and this lass wanted to know where the club was,' he explained. 'She has come all the way from Edinburgh,' he added. 'Can we have two pints of lager, please?' The woman grinned and said nothing. She considered his explanation as she turned the taps. It was plausible, she supposed. Just then a huge blast of feedback from downstairs announced that the band was about to start. It was going to be one hell of a night. More people were coming through the door.

Clive turned around when he spotted the Russian woman – a friend of Judd, surely – stroll in. What was this gal doing in town? She seemed to have turned up not that long after Judd showed but he did not seem to have any time for her.

She turned around and walked over; blinking those very blue eyes, 'Should be good tonight,' she held out her hand and for a moment he thought he might kiss it.

'Indeed, Comrade,' he said.

'When does it start?' Anya asked.

'Not long – 10 pm,' he said.

'I like what I hear,' returned Anya.

'You a big fan of reggae?' Clive quizzed.

Anya responded, 'My niece said they were famous.' 'She's a student at St Andrews, studying Russian folk music.'

Clive frowned. 'I didn't know reggae had got to Russia'

Monica overheard them talking, from behind the bar. Anya continued, 'I am actually the Scottish correspondent for RT. It's a London based TV channel.'

'Really?' he said. 'Well, I never.' Tell that to the horse marines! To be honest, he was surprised, she did not seem like a journalist, he had even thought she might be a model; Russian? Well, maybe. What a bizarre conversation.

Just then Pablo announced that he was taking tickets for the band downstairs. They both joined it. He was surprised to see Beth on the door. Soon after, she said, 'Tickets, please.' They both handed their slips over and joined the throng descending the stairs.

Judd was at the back of the stage. He needed to get out of this place right away, before anyone realised what he had on him. He would have to act punter first because if he left now it might look suspicious. He looked up and there was Anya coming down the stairs, along with Clive. Damn! Why had he not got here earlier, done the business, as Pablo had cautioned and been long gone? This was most unfortunate. He would need to make some excuse but what? He had the rucksack on his back, he made a dash for the toilets hoping they would not see him.

And they didn't. It was empty. He looked around for a hiding place. The toilet cisterns had a diagonal shelf screwed on top; probably to discourage cocaine users. He noticed the red electrical tape around the cistern pipework – another botch job then. Maybe there was a cleaners' cupboard – yes, there was one and – better still – it was open. He furiously shovelled the rucksack under a pile of toilet rolls and hurried back to the gig.

What was he going to say now? Consternation swept across his face. He needed to tell Pablo. This time they spotted him straightaway. He decided to lead the conversation – maybe the band would start playing and drown out the need for small talk.

'Anya, Clive, what a surprise!' Clive did not smile.

'Hello, Judd, you come down for the gig?

'Oh, yes, love it.' Anya nodded. Clive frowned. He had never thought of his stepbrother as a music aficionado. Never mind.

Chapter 8

(500)

Monica was Beth's friend behind the bar. It was a second job for her, as she worked at a holistic magazine, called "Namastaia". This was a small all-girl outfit, which had been started by a local chiropractor. It ran articles on mindfulness and other spiritual practices – reiki, yoga, Zumba and so on.

She had taken the bar job because her day-job did not pay much. Namastaia was a not for profit organisation, she was their advertising manager. She admired what Pablo had achieved in such a small market town. She was also a musician, a singer-songwriter and hoped to start an open mike night one day.

She had been joined by Pablo but had lost Beth. They really should have gotten more staff tonight and she knew Pablo would soon vanish again when the band started up. She could only suppose money must be tight. They were late starting (yet again), as bands so often were. It was getting on for 10:30. There should be fewer drinkers once they started. Oh well. 'Another pint, Mike?' she asked.

Pablo came over. 'Back downstairs, hun, you can manage up here, eh?'

Pablo bounded on to the stage downstairs, to introduce the band. 'I want to say, to everyone here, thank you so much for coming here tonight. I know some of you have come from far and away. You will see one of the biggest bands from Jamaica right here, on their way to tour the rest of the country. Please put your hands together to welcome Yellowman!'

The unmistakeable albino Rastafarian then strode on stage, as the drummer let off a fusillade on his tom-toms. A dance hall veteran in his late sixties, Yellowman had an immediate stage presence as he was an albino Rastafarian. The band charged into their first number. Reggae takes its unique sound from playing on the off-beat, plus the unusual time signatures. The dancehall material was unfamiliar to most of the locals. The hardcore fans down from Edinburgh knew better and it rocked. Pablo was recording the sound and streaming it out on the Omegaplex's Facebook page. The expression "hit the ground running" sprang to mind. Anya was having a lithe boogie while Clive and Judd looked on. He thought she looked really good with her leather pants and a white blouse.

Upstairs, Monica only had a handful of customers; there were a few married couples on a night out, the ex-racing correspondent at the bar and the miserable alcoholic in the corner whose name she had never wanted to know, so she walked out to the stair hall. Beth still had a few tickets left.

'No turn always yet, then?'

'No, it was early days yet.'

Back at the bar, Monica felt it would be a good night. She looked at her watch – 11 pm. She was glad that she was not cleaning up tomorrow, they would probably not finish until two am at the earliest and the bar would not close until one am. There would be a late surge, no doubt, many more beers yet to be sold, hopefully, Beth would have sold all the tickets by then and could join her back at the bar. She might have to ask Pablo to change the odd barrel.

Chapter 9

(2a)

Anya was enjoying herself. The crowd were swaying around the stage in time to the beats. The bass thudded through her chest and the percussion was hypnotic. There did seem to be a lot of bass in reggae. Clive was standing back against the wall, along with Judd, who, she thought, seemed out of sorts.

'I need to speak to Pablo, bro, back in a minute.' He shrugged, why did Judd have to be here – spoiling the party. He did not want to talk to his stepbrother anyway, Judd forced his way over to the sound booth. Pablo waved him off. He stormed up the stairs and out into the night.

Clive was pleased to see Judd go. He reminded of him as a child, it wasn't easy. He also wondered why he had managed to piss Beth off, it seemed to happen to him all the time. He would see his dad on Wednesday and have a chat about that, something was not right. Enough. He stepped out on to the dance floor. Maybe Beth could be persuaded to come and join in one day. He smiled. Then he remembered she was at work, upstairs.

Chapter 10

(S£o)

It was Sunday morning. Martin let himself in, as he did every Sunday to clean up the mess left on the night (and morning) earlier. He had walked in from Muirside on the outskirts of town. At least it was not raining. Holy mother of god what a mess! What he saw was sour beer, cigarette butts, even the odd broken glass. He trudged wearily down the stairs to the cleaner's cupboard. Pablo was no doubt deep asleep in the upstairs flat. The bar staff had not even managed to wash up all the glasses, but that was not his problem, they did not open on Sunday anyway.

Where to do start? Brush and broom, a thumping rhythm, followed by a wash bucket, then vacuum the carpets. Leave the loos till last, working back to his cupboard. This could take hours! He picked up the broom and a sheaf of bin bags; he would work from upstairs down, he decided. He better put his rubber gloves on what with all this glass all over the place.

Meanwhile, Judd had slept badly. He had rung Pablo all morning but there was no reply, he was obviously out for the count. The band had been put up by his friends in a nearby village. They would be on their way out of Newcastleton anytime today, then en-route to Liverpool where they had been booked for a Monday night gig. Newcastleton was where they were lodging tonight. Meanwhile, his stash was mouldering away in the cleaner's cupboard and didn't they have a cleaner who came on Sunday morning? There was no other solution, he would have to get around there right now.

Martin had finished the bar area and started on the stairs. All of a sudden there was a massive hammering on the door. *Who the hell could this be, there were never any deliveries on a Sunday*? He went over to the front door and stared through the peephole. Yes, it was one of the regulars, though not one he had spoken to. He unbolted the door.

'What do you want?' he asked.

'I left my bag here last night, came to collect it.'

Martin frowned. 'Look, mate, I'm just the cleaner, come back on Monday when we are open.'

'No, you don't understand it has my wallet in it.'

Martin thought. 'Well, I haven't found any bags, mate, where did you think you left it?'

'It might have been the toilets.'

'Well, they're not cleaned yet.' Then Judd forced the door open and bounded past Martin. He chased him down the stairs. He got a rugby tackle on him just inside the gents. Judd made for the cupboard and got the door open. A pungent smell of cannabis suddenly filled the atmosphere. 'So that's your game, sonny!' Martin understood exactly what was going down here. 'Give me one reason I shouldn't call the police.'

Judd sweated. 'Let's do a deal, you didn't see anything…and I cut you in 10%. What do you think?'

'In your dreams,' Judd winced. Now he would have to have that talk with Anya.

'What would it take tonight?' Judd reached in his pocket, he had about £200 in his wallet. 'Here, take this and we can both walk away.'

Martin thought he would agree – why drag the police in, he could lose his job. The club might be shut down.

'Let's have it then.'

Judd handed him his wad. He would have to have a word with Pablo come Monday. Judd was up the stairs with the rucksack and he heard the front door slam. *What a shit*. Martin winced and carried on with the cleaning.

Chapter 11

(250)

Pablo was furious with Judd. The club had not opened because it was the Monday following a very good weekend's taking and he had been in a buoyant mood. 'Look, sonny – there will be no more deals done on these premises. I trusted you. You have truly screwed up. You know the house rule. What if Martin talks?'

Judd said, 'I got cold feet when my brother Clive came in. He had that Russian floosie with him, and I don't trust her.' He did not, of course, mention that she had already sussed his game out. 'I should have sorted it earlier.'

'Yes, you should've. That Anya woman, the one with the husky? You mean she isn't genuine?' He paused and scratched his beard. 'Well, this is what she told me, she is the Scottish correspondent for RT, that TV channel on Freeview. What would she know anyway?'

Judd was even more alarmed. 'I never knew that!' He paused to think. 'That wasn't what she told me. I still want to carry on, no more drops here obviously. Perhaps choose somewhere out of town, out of any oversight, then we can do it where nobody will see us, somewhere like the moor beyond Newcastleton?'

Pablo nodded. 'I see your drift, the backcountry where we might be out of sight?'

'OK, my jeep can get up those hill tracks, I doubt the bands will mind a picnic up there.' The military relic still had its uses.

'Let me have a word with Martin soon, the next Jamaican band are due over next weekend.' He would have to put up a front or Martin might go to the police. He would have to play the gangster. He sighed.

Chapter 12

(250)

Rochelle opened the caravan door. The site was quiet as none of the other travellers were awake yet. There was not a cloud in the sky. Her parents were asleep in the caravan. She lit her cigarette, thinking, *One day I will escape from this place.*

The traveller site was a few miles out of town, a group of thirty-odd caravans sandwiched between the motorway and an electricity sub-station. There was horse pasture in the field next door. It had once been a private caravan park but the council had bought it up and added amenity blocks and a community centre. Kids had a pony and trap, which they ran around the estate.

She had been seeing the Russian for the last month. She seemed to be someone important, unlike other wastrels she knew in the gypsy community. She was due to meet her at the club on Saturday night. What a strange name – Anya, she thought. She must be rich – weren't all Russians?

Every day, she added a note to her diary, especially if anything good happened; but lately, she could not think of anything to write. Maybe she was depressed?

She needed to do her laundry. The site washer was broken, so she needed to go into town and call in at Rosie's laundrette. Maybe she would bump into Anya there? That would be exciting. Not likely though. She discarded the butt and went back to her caravan.

She felt stifled, she tried not to allow herself to feel hopeless, but she was seething internally. Who was sticking up to people like her? Get the kettle on, then get out. The bus stop was just up the road.

28

Chapter 13

(358)

Monica was meeting her younger brother Morton after work. He was doing his AS levels in sixth form college. They had always been close as children. They were in her flat.

'You see, Morton, it is quite a difficult line to tread.' He looked surprised. They were talking about the world of work and the magazine that Monica worked for, Namastaia. How she juggled two jobs to make ends meet.

'Sis, not great to have this diagnosis. They now think I'm never going to achieve much now!' Morton was getting frustrated. 'That's why I signed up for Climate Extinction.'

'Not good enough, Morton. Yes, it's hard but you have to accept it. You are my brother, I will not let you go down. Ruin your weekend, if you want!'

'You don't have a reputation to lose, you only have a reputation to make.' he continued. 'I am still at school and you totally underestimate how hard it is going to be. What am I going to achieve in this dismal northern town? What are the three biggest employers? A call centre, Biscuits, tyres, the NHS?'

'Come on, Morton.' She shook her head. 'I know you find your Asperger's a nuisance, but you have got a lot more potential than that. You can get away to university, travel around. You have skills other people do not. There are loads of jobs in construction, manufacturing and financial services, because of a skills' shortage and a paucity of qualifications – '

'And lazy corporations and vested interests, we are supposed to have the power to elect the people, who set the way we are governed and we have the power of consumers to control and change what can be sold to us…but I'm afraid most of us have been practically wilfully ignorant and have put very short-term convenience and pleasures above the future of our children. Sis, I tell you, I used to drink at that Omegaplex place, even though I was underage. If I stay here, I will end up on drugs, just like a few of my friends.'

'Which friends? You know what I think? Few kids have done manual labour, they don't have either the discipline or social skills.'

'Well, a few in Muirside, won't say more than that. Wherever you're going, wherever you've been. You've been there before and you'll be there again.'

She shook her head. This was not what she wanted to hear from her brother. It was a different generation, to be sure. It was like he had become a stranger.

Chapter 14

(250)

Clive was drawing up some plans for a hotel extension, but in reality, his mind was far away. It was a long day in the office and he was in a pensive mood. His face showed an unhealthy pallor by the computer monitor, mirroring his mood.

He had pencilled in Johnny Hashback, a Johnny Cash cover artist he had heard about, he apparently came from Oban, for his first open mike. His Facebook page told him he was to be on tour in England but would be passing through Frackburgh on his way down to England the week after next. Monica would swap the bar for the mixing desk. He would square it with Pablo, who was sure to be up for it, he thought.

He had a lot of phoning around to do. He had never been a music promoter before. He been down the print shop and had plastered A5 posters around the town. Perhaps even traditional folkies would turn up? That would be good.

He turned back to his work, the coloured lines on the screen coming back into focus. It should be more fun than this. It paid the bills though. Opportunities were scarce in this hollowed-out shell of a town. Biscuits and tyres were the main employers; he had overcome a lot to get so far, architecture school and his dad moving up here to escape his relationship. But then, on the minus side, Judd had followed.

Chapter 15

(200)

The laundrette was quiet, a frozen moment in the day, as Rochelle stuffed in her clothing. The room smelled of cold soap and drainage. The coins went in the slot one by one, the soap powder in the hopper. She had come into town after another fruitless argument with her father, who had had a go at her when he woke up as she put the kettle on. He was trying to pair her up with another family-approved match on the site. No Neanderthal bride would she be. She squirmed inwardly, she was reluctant to tell him of her lesbian feelings because she would surely be shown the door. It was so depressing. All she wanted to do was get away from this place

Her wash had finished. She transferred it to the tumble dryer. The load rose and fell, round and round in the tumbler, she could feel the heat.

She decided she would give Anya a ring, meet her in town for a coffee. She fancied her. *What was she doing today?* Rochelle wondered. What did a journalist do all day? She went outdoors for a fag. She got out her phone. She got through on the fourth ring. 'Anya, hi, are you in town? Fancy a coffee and a chat?'

Chapter 16

(356)

Monica was at work in the Namastaia offices. She was three weeks away from the copy date for the next issue of the magazine. This involved ringing around her database of past and present advertisers to tempt them to take a box advert for events or services in the classified listings in the magazine. One of the large publishers always had the back page of the magazine – a big sell at £1200 – without her advertising revenue, they could not afford to go to press. Printers saw them as high risk and wanted cash on the nail. The articles were written by leading lights of the mindfulness movement, who worked from the front of the magazine, generally for free, while she worked backwards. In two weeks, they would meet in the middle and there would be an awkward bit of juggling to compose the "cut" She enjoyed it all. The outside world might well be an epidemic of anxiety and despair but not in here. She smiled and returned to her work.

The great excitement in the office was that a famous Buddhist monk, Mahinuata, was going to speak about his spiritual beliefs. He came from the nearby monastery *San-u-delin*. The talk was to be held at Frackburgh assembly rooms the following month. Now the mission was to get the word out and sell a bit of advertising at the same time.

This was the only monastery in the border area, some miles north of the upland pasture where (unbeknown to her) the club would be conducting the illicit business of a weekend. Monica had spoken to the monastery to see if the magazine could carry an advertisement for the talk.

She had also decided to contact Anya whom she had learnt from the bar conversation, worked for RT, the TV channel. She was not sure whether they would be interested but it was potentially regional TV coverage. What a stroke of luck! She picked up the phone. Made that next call.

Chapter 17

(466)

Clive was on site. Local contractors Strongarm Construction were extending the homeless hostel. It was opposite the biscuit factory. He was here to attend a site meeting. He was becoming increasingly frustrated by the "make do and mend" attitude to work, he would have to raise this in the meeting, which he realised could be used as a bargaining chip.

They were not even employing a site engineer, so the foundations had been all over the place, they had put extra ring beams in place to make sure there was proper support for the walls. He went into the site office.

'Brent, why are all the plastic weep-holes all bright yellow when we have red brickwork?'

The site agent looked up to his eye level. 'Well, did you put red weep-holes on the drawing?'

Clive sighed. 'I don't tell you what size nails you use, do I?' He could not raise make and mend now at the meeting, as he had intended. He would have to be extra careful from now on, he would have to accept what they had put in. Why did he have to be the fall guy for a contractor whose buyer shopped around for the cheapest deal?

He went into the site cabin. They were all seated around the conference table – site manager, contracts manager and the council bod. He took his seat. The agendas had been handed out.

'Can we start with documentation?'

'Have the heads of agreement been witnessed?'

His mind had drifted to musical matters. He had a friend who worked at citizens advice, who knew all the local bands. He had also been on the internet, but it was difficult to tell from a webpage how local they were. Perhaps some were clients of his? He now had that list and was going to ring or Facebook them in the next few days and see if there was any interest in a charity gig or, failing that, open mike. Pablo would welcome the extra trade at the bar. Maybe he could get some tuition in any case?

Everyone was staring at him.

'Clive?'

He realised he had not been paying attention.

'When can we get these signed?'

He thought. 'Next week,' he said.

He returned to the office. Some jobs go well, some were seemingly doomed from day one. This was that one. Was it all down to the luck of the draw? The jury was out. His employer did not even pay him until the seventh of the month following the month he worked. He was fed up. He would go straight to the club when he was finished.

He saw Monica alone at the bar and made a small conversation with her. She seemed interested in his proposition. She had popped in after work too.

'Could we start an open mike and meet more of the local musicians up here, say a trial run?'

She paused. 'I think so. We will need help, you know, publicity too, but I can play guitar and you could go on the mixing desk. I could teach you that.'

'What about learning the instrument?' he asked. 'That would take a lot of time and effort.'

She replied nodding, 'Yes, it took me two years. But you could do it one number at a time, that would build up your confidence.'

'I have been pottering around with the guitar for a year. I will pick one number I like and work on it up then,' he replied.

'Thanks.'

She ran her fingers up his arms, like stroking a cat. It was seductive.

Chapter 18

(266)

That evening, Martin responded to his summons and came into Pablo's inner sanctum. He had rung Martin, as he had agreed with Judd, to ask him to pop in. He had not gone into any details. He offered him the chair opposite him. 'We need to talk.'

He accepted the chair opposite Pablo.

'Before you start, I know what happened.'

'How?' Pablo did not wait for a response and continued, 'Have you ever figured out how this club pays its way?'

Understanding dawned on Martin. 'Yes. I see.'

'You saw something you didn't need to see. You didn't see anything, OK. Your job is secure here. Your silence would be welcomed. I recommend you consider that.'

Martin nodded. He mouthed, 'OK.' He walked away out of the door, thinking. *I don't think this has ended yet, not by a long chalk. I will make my move when I decide.*

It was the strangest conversation he had ever had with any employer. He shook his head, it was plain inadequate, just bewildering.

Chapter 19

(500)

Pablo's jeep rumbled over the rough track. He was heading up to the abandoned Pele tower on the borderland. With him was Judd. Pablo was not in the best of moods as he thought about the Godfather speech he had given to Martin. He was desperately trying to diversify the business and had bought a second-hand pizza oven. He had to get a takeaway licence but before that, he needed to get the kitchen up to scratch. How would he ever free himself from this gravy train? He liked taking risks, oh yes, but never like this.

The lowering gloom was palpable, a thunderstorm imminent. At least there was no one about on the moors, just grazing cattle. In the evening, someone would come and herd them up from the common-land and take them back to their home farms. Judd winced as they hit another pothole on the way. The shock absorbers would need changing with any more of this, thought Pablo.

They had exchanged no words on the entire journey. Judd wanted to remind him that he had lost £200 as well but bit his tongue.

The rendezvous was a mere ten minutes away, halfway between Frackburgh and Newcastleton. He had made the call on an unregistered mobile. He was lucky to get a signal – one bar! This cattle pasture, on the moorland, had been there for centuries, a boggy mire which was now part Scottish and part English, the scene of many a skirmish by Border Reivers over a long period of disputed possession. Come Scottish union, they had built a dyke across the middle, this was known as the Scotch dyke, for no apparent reason, ironic, since it had been built by the English.

There were few settlements of any kind, making it the ideal place for this exchange, in a zone long party to smuggling and cattle rustling. Pablo was still furious, Judd could tell. To him, it was all about music, the means and the ends. To Judd, it was just a means of living. It was better paid than car dealing, anyway.

They had told the band there could be a picnic, but that was yesterday. It was hardly the right weather, not here, not today. They would do the "drop" as quickly as possible and head off in different directions, to avoid any suspicion. He caught sight of a red car in the distance. The rendezvous was around the corner. They pulled up alongside with a scrunch of tyres. 'Yo!' Drops of rain started to fall.

'Let's get this done.'

Martin pulled out a bundle of fifty-pound notes, a thousand pounds.

'See you on Saturday!' Tranor laughed.

'Windrush retribution, honky! You had the faith, we know the score, Rastafari. We love you honkies.'

The swag bag was handed over.

'See you back in Frackburgh.'

The band had parked their van at their B and B in Newcastleton and was then headed north to Edinburgh on Sunday evening. Pablo and Judd headed south, back down to the club.

Chapter 20

Pablo wasn't sure. It was later the same day. Clive had broached the possibility of a Tuesday night slot for the open mike, chatting at the bar. There was a frown on his face when he mentioned Johnny Hashback. Clive queried this. 'What have you heard about him? Isn't he any good?'

'I am sure you could find somebody more local to play a Johnny Cash cover.'

Clive was puzzled. Did Pablo think he was muscling in on his promotions? Surely not! 'But you have bands come all the way from Jamaica!' he exclaimed.

'Yes but they are the real thing. Just get some local musicians to help you.'

He turned and walked away, frowning. Perhaps he was worried about expenses then? Pablo was in no mood for persuasion, that much was clear.

He shook his head, he would ring up Monica for advice. He didn't want to spoil his good luck. He got his mobile out. 'Hi, Mon. You know that first act I wanted to book, seems like Pablo has taken a dislike to him, says we should get someone more local.' She seemed surprised. 'Well, I don't know him, of course, but you could email him and ask if he needs travel expenses.'

'Where did you get the name from?' she queried.

'I found it on the web.'

Her mind drifted back to when she had met Paul on Tinder. He had dumped her soon enough and now her younger sister, Kate, was dating her ex-boyfriend. She frowned, it was beyond the pall, how could a sister do that? *We all live in our own shells*, she mused. She would try and give Clive her full support, he was a lovely man. She put that dark thought behind her. She must not mention her sister at all. Clive, after all, had the courage to initiate this music night.

Clive thought they had been cut off. 'Are you still there?' he asked.

'Sorry, er...my mind was elsewhere. Look I will get you some local musician friends instead. Just forget this Cash bloke.'

Chapter 21

Rochelle had arranged to meet Anya on the market square at "Beanz for Us" for a coffee, which featured outside tables where she could have a smoke. Pigeons strutted across the square. She wanted to talk about getting a job. Anya did not smoke and shivered in the faint sunlight. Rochelle had her laundry bag with her.

Rochelle told her about life on a traveller site, the family culture, the family feuds and the lack of respect for women. 'Tell me all about your life, Anya.'

'Being a journalist is not as great as it might seem, Rochelle. There is no routine, you have to be able to go anywhere over the whole of Scotland and the border, at a moment's notice, always on call. We work every other weekend and then get time off in the week, like today.' Yesterday, I had to go all the way to Stranraer, it's a long way to travel there and back.'

'That sounds really interesting, my routine is boring me to death,' she replied. 'A few of my friends have joined the army. Jimmy has just left like you have to, they kick them out at 45. He is always banging on about civvy street.'

'He sounds stuck, you mean? He is lost.'

'They always tell you what to do. Now he drives around looking for scrap metal. He has seen some terrible things, that's for sure – Northern Ireland, Iraq.'

'Well, ENOUGH OF THAT, what do you want to do?'

'Maybe get a job,' she replied. 'Some independent income would be good, get out of this town, anyway.'

'The grass is always greener on the other side,' Anya laughed. 'Don't run away, Rochelle. No one is losing sleep over your intellectual development, are they?' she said.

'Instead, they have emptied your mind with superficialities.'
She made a gesture with her hands. 'Time for you to take
back control. Ambition is doing the right thing, you know.'
She nodded her head knowingly.

Rochelle nodded her head slowly and took a long drag.
Well, at least she had a new mission in life. It was true that
gypsies were treated like pondlife. It was time to leave.

Chapter 22

Scull listened to Monica play some Travis. It was something about rivers, oceans and driftwood. He liked it, apparently, they came from Glasgow. It was one he vaguely recognised, but more modern than the traditional stuff he was used to playing on guitar. He normally went to a monthly folk club but had been attracted here by a poster he had seen in the town library. He was quite impressed. There was a young man on the mixing desk. It was a Wednesday evening, midweek.

He joined the others applauding her performance. She got up to speak again. 'Thank you for coming to this gig. I hope to do this regularly, maybe even weekly, if the interest is there. Now, Clive is going to play his first-ever solo number.' She went over to the mixing desk, shooting a smile of encouragement.

Clive came up to the mike. He looked nervous, he was struggling to change chords as it was and said hesitantly, 'I haven't played this in public before, so bear with me.' With a forced grin, he set into a song about a relationship and the risk and fears of it all, fluffing the odd note on the way. Nobody seemed to mind, though.

At last, he had finished. He was sweating with the concentration. There was widespread applause. Monica smiled from behind the mixing desk. Scull asked Clive, 'Is that one of yours?'

'I wish,' Clive said. 'It is by Bastille.' Scull had never heard of them and just smiled. It wasn't really folk at all. He had agreed to play later on and he had decided to play some traditional folk – Lindisfarne – also a number about a river – Fog on the Tyne. He felt duty-bound to help out as there were only a handful of musicians there. Apparently, it was the first time they had run this, but the sound was crystal clear down here in the basement. They knew what they were doing.

He had enjoyed himself, it was something new and he would come again. The others were getting their gear together and he asked as he got up to leave, 'When are you meeting next?'

'Come back this time next week,' was the reply from Clive. 'We would welcome your support, thank you.'

Monica made an announcement, 'Please, sign up for our email list.'

Clive and Monica went back up the stairs to the bar. Pablo was polishing glasses. 'Well done guys, you sounded good and you brought us some new punters!' Scull shook his hand. At last, something had been given back to him by his punters. There was a bad vibe in the bar, though.

At the bar, she noticed a woman called Karen, she was letting off some steam and drinking. She was talking to Rochelle. It was unusual to see her here on a weekday. What was going on? Clive took it to be an altercation.

'So you think you are so much better than me; just because of that lousy job at some call centre.'

'Not at all, Karen. If you want to spend your entire life as a gypsy bride then that's your choice. But not me.'

Karen was all piercings and dagger-like looks. 'I came here to talk some sense into you. We all worry about you.'

Rochelle parried. 'And what would you know about that? You are too out of your face most of the time.'

'That's good coming from you. You've scrubbed up well. We call you the queen of hearts. They all asked me what your fallback position is.'

'Not men, Karen.'

Rochelle really felt her antipathy. She had to wonder, did her fellow campers really see her as a threat to their social order, to their men? It was pointless arguing. Turbulent feelings wrenched at her. She picked up her coat and said,

'Look after yourself, Karen.' She wagged her finger. 'I'm off now.' Pearls before swine.

Clive turned through the door to let her pass, paused and thought – well, a different world up here, but shame anyway on Pablo for his earlier lack of support for a guest artist then. Still, he had to admit, it had gone alright, even if it had been nerve-racking.

Clive noticed the confrontation. In addition, a shoplifter had also come in to sell his bargain half-price packs of gammon. Only Karen seemed interested; locally shoplifted, he was sure.

Monica hugged Clive and they parted their ways. They had done enough, better than up here. He could hold his head up high. He would be off to his dad's for dinner tomorrow.

Pablo scowled. He had not enjoyed this evening. He should bar the shoplifter. You had no choice in this job. One step forward, one back.

Chapter 23

Roy was sitting at the kitchen table, reading the local rag. He had just come back from work a few minutes earlier. It was harder to work now that he was in a wheelchair, but the mobility vehicle had helped. He was a grocery buyer.

'I see that nightclub in town is applying for a takeaway licence. It says here they want to do pizza deliveries.'

Greta was cooking on the farmhouse range. 'They are being ambitious then.'

'If you ask me, looks a dodgy set-up to me, but fair play to have a go, I suppose,' said Roy. 'Is our son coming soon?'

'Six o'clock,' Greta replied. 'He told me he organised an open mike there last night.'

Roy frowned, that was where Judd drank too, wasn't it? Perhaps he felt the way he did because of Judd.

He heard the front door open.

'Anyone home?'

It was Clive all right. Roy called, 'How did it go?'

'Oh, you mean, the open mike? I was so nervous, but there was a good turnout.' Roy smiled, 'Winners all round then?'

'Monica, she works behind the bar, couldn't have done it without her, she was a star.'

Greta had filled the kettle and was waiting for it to boil. She announced the meal would be ready shortly – a rich stew. Clive sat down in the settee and turned to his dad. 'Busy day at the office?'

'Always, as a buyer. These supermarkets drive a hard bargain.'

They sat down to eat. Clive asked, 'Did I tell you Judd was there last Saturday?'

'Really?' Roy quizzed. 'I don't know why he hangs around there. Is he really a music fan?'

'He didn't come to my open mike anyway,' he laughed.

Why do I think about him at all? Roy thought.

'Why spend so much time worrying about him?' Clive asked.

Because I'm his father, thought Roy. He said nothing, it was hopeless. He changed the subject. 'How's your work going?'

'Oh, pretty routine, if you want to know,' he smiled. 'We keep bidding for larger projects but we don't seem to get them. I am looking at a new housing co-op, I am applying to be a non-executive director.'

His dad nodded his encouragement but he still was not listening.

'Dad, why do I piss off women so easily? It seems to happen to me all the time.'

'Well, it's what some women do. We need to talk about the things that make us uncomfortable, I agree.'

Greta shook her head and said, 'Don't forget Louise is joining us next weekend.' All this talk was a nuisance to her, broken stones from previous times never quite going away. She preferred to hear from her own daughter, who had never held her new love against her.

Chapter 24

Rochelle had heard that a new call centre was opening on Frackburgh business park and eagerly put her name forward. Anya had planted the seed. The money would be useful. She desperately needed to make something of her life, leave the suffocating traveller culture, which for her as a woman, was very restricting. Anya had encouraged her to take this step, she was a genuine friend. She was a real person after all. She walked into the job shop, an agency run by the council. She would do it.

'Yes. Letisea Telecom is taking on a new batch of fifteen new staff, which they do every quarter, and the induction will be this Friday,' the man behind the counter said.

'What does it involve?' she queried.

'Making and receiving calls in an open-plan office,' he said. 'Is your CV up to date?'

'Er, no I don't have one, actually, but I have worked behind the bar.'

A smile crossed his face. 'Don't worry, we can get one put together, I can make an appointment for you with an adviser to put one together.'

She needed to show some enthusiasm so agreed. She would do the training and hope for the best. How hard could it be?

'It isn't ever going to be easy,' she said to herself as she walked away quickly.

Chapter 25

Martin had finished his mid-week cleaning at the Omegaplex. He had come from his girlfriend's house. It was Wednesday evening. He was talking to Beth behind the bar after he had finished up. 'So this guy coming to town, Mah something, is he the real deal? Tell me more about Buddhism.'

Beth smiled. 'Oh, its Monica you really need to talk to, she is the real Buddhist 'round here. Well, it's a very spiritual practice,' she started. 'Monica is always on about it, I believe it to be a complete belief system, in fact; why not come along and have a listen?'

Just then, Judd came in off the street. He winced. Their eyes met. Would there be a scene? Well, a deal is a deal. 'We were talking about Buddhism, actually,' Judd said. Well, he had to say something. It sounded false to him. Beth winked at him as if to say don't.

Martin was conflicted, anything to get away at this point. There must be more to life than Muirside, battleship grey concrete blocks plonked on sphagnum moss or this damned club and its dirty linen. Council property – flats, houses, libraries, school playgrounds, youth clubs, all sold off and profited from. He was ready to cut and run if this was required.

Judd took it in his stride. Martin was surprised when he said, 'Yes, we are all thinking of going, so why not come along?' Martin was shocked. So was it all an act, like nothing had happened? He would never understand human beings as long as he lived. Judd carried on, 'Well, as you say, how often do you get to see a real Buddhist 'round this neck of the woods?' They all laughed.

He finally said, 'OK, count me in.' Why waste time being angry, what was it to him? A £200 windfall? He did feel curious about Buddhism though, so he would accept their unexpected offer. Judd ordered a pint, while Martin left to return home.

It was a strange day in a strange town he thought, but time to go, as he walked back to the bus stop. Another day, another dollar?

Chapter 26

Pablo opened the envelope and scanned through the contents. He had apparently been summoned for jury service. He had to attend the Crown Court for a whole fortnight, Monday to Friday, starting next week. This would play havoc with running the business.

He would have to ask Beth, Martin and Monica to put in extra hours during the weekday evenings, he thought. Martin would need to serve behind the bar, take deliveries and cover for when Beth and Monica were unavailable. What rotten timing, bad for the bottom line too.

He put his head in his hands. It was bad news. He had traded all his hopes and dreams for this venture. Denise would not be pleased as it would be a nightmare to cover for the kids.

Chapter 27

Jimmie Armstrong was on his way to the betting office in Muirside. There were few people hanging around. It was mid-afternoon and the races were starting. He trudged down the grim stairwell of his tower block. The lift was out of order, again. He lived on the top floor of Bellingham Tower, a tenth-floor view was his only compensation. That and his love of gambling, that is.

Three years ago, they had kicked him out of the army as they did when you are over the hill; he had fallen in with his scrap 'round by default. That was how he had got to know Judd, the used car dealer. He had already got the habit in the barracks. You couldn't have supported addiction on scrap metal, though. His own father had been Italian, he had been interned during the war at a prisoner of war camp on the outskirts of the town. He had met a local girl and stayed in the town. She had left and Dad was long since dead.

His flat had become the stash for Judd, it was an arrangement that suited them well because it meant Jimmie never set foot in the club. The supply chain was secure. He had the strongest front door, sheet steel, no PVC for him. Civvy street was rubbish. But his sideline paid, oh yes. Now for a spot of snooker down the stick hall, then he was going to the races.

He did have competition, though. Not that Anya knew about. Not that Pablo did either. He frowned. Angus was a rival on the estate. Not a problem for him, though. In fact, he lived in the same building and pretended to ignore him.

It was a Friday race day afternoon and Jimmy fancied a flutter on the real thing. Frackburgh had an established racecourse, located on the more opulent south-west side of the town. Going there was a somewhat theatrical event. He sometimes met with the racing correspondent there who had worked for the local paper. He often had valuable inside information, knowing the jockeys and the vets. Gambling was exciting and he felt the adrenalin as the race started. 'Is it going to be a good day, Kenneth?'

'Every race depends on the going; it's nice and firm today.' He continued, 'And the runners of course.'

He laughed and volunteered, 'And I should know. So who have you in mind?'

'My money is on Carrimore,' he continued. 'He is a newbie, a chancer maybe, a plucky fellow, but the odds will be good. Because he is a first-timer, he will be wearing blinkers, which could make the difference. He is also drawn on the inside, in stall one.'

'Thanks, that's helpful, I will give it a go. It's always going to be a question of luck.' He grinned. But maybe he was too calculating to be a gambler? Betting is nothing to do with equality you have to take risks!

'A horse is like a bigger dog, you know, Jimmie. It all depends on the jockey.' Kenneth chuckled. Jimmy frowned, was he being serious? Kenneth had a wry sense of humour. Had he placed too much faith in this tipster?

Chapter 28

Anya was in the market square, having a coffee with Maya, who was a member of the Forward Intelligence Unit, part of her back-up team. She had been covertly photographing all the coming and goings at the club and the data was going into the criminal database. Anya was in the process of putting names against the faces. Maya took the mugshots by pretending to be waving her phone around on the other side of the pavement from the club.

'Maya, we need to be vigilant. If we are seen to be targeting the Omegaplex then it will blow our cover. If I was a real journalist, I might have some excuse. Then I could do an advertorial feature, but there you go.'

Maya nodded, 'I understand, softly-softly.'

'I only want you to take one photo a day, spread it out, OK? Oh, and avoid eye contact with the punters.'

'OK.'

This was how she had come to focus on Judd, who always came in on a Saturday morning, regular as clockwork. Because she was based away from the office, she needed to view photos on a memory stick. This was not legal, but occasionally you had to bend the rules. This was allowed, apparently.

Also in the square, that morning was an English Nationalist stall. It was ironic, she thought, for a town with so few immigrants.

Chapter 29

The bar was filling up as it could be sure to do to every Saturday. Rochelle was pleased to get out of the caravan site. The warden had asked her if she had seen Jimmy lately as some debt collector had turned looking for his pick-up truck. She said no, she hadn't. The band had arrived and was tuning up downstairs. Apparently, Monica had said, a guy called Jules had set up a stall in the gents, somehow promoting men's gels. How had he wormed his way in? Did Pablo even know?

Anya was already drinking at the bar with her vodka and tonic. They had met yesterday and had a good old chinwag. They hugged, while Beth looked on. The satellite TV was beaming some obscure European match. Kenneth, the ex-racing correspondent was studying the form. He seemed to be using Pablo's computer. Her darling Marilyn was again sleeping over with Denise.

'Do we know when the band is on?' Anya quizzed.

'Ask Pablo,' Beth replied. 'We never know ourselves with these bands. At least "Da Kingston Boys" are here.' She added, 'And at least we have got more staff in tonight.' Turning to Martin, who for the first time was behind the bar, 'Monica's here too,' Beth added.

'I've been promoted,' he beamed. 'But I will be back in to clean up from you lot tomorrow, so keep it tidy.' Martin laughed and they joined in. 'Now what are you having, I need to get some practice in pulling a pint. So what will it be, Rochelle?' he asked.

Rochelle said she would let him know. There was general laughter.

Monica turned to Beth and asked, 'Is Clive coming tonight?'

She pulled a face. 'We fell out last weekend, but expect he will though.' Monica had just changed a barrel and had come back up the stairs. She saw Anya perched on a barstool next to Rochelle. She remembered the difficult conversation she had with Clive about her Catholic orphanage.

Could it be an opportune moment to broach the Mahinua workshop, she wondered? She would give it a try anyway. Perhaps best to make it a general remark to both of them?

'Did you guys know we have a Buddhist monastery just ten miles away?' she queried. Anya seemed surprised. She had no idea there were Buddhists in this country. 'No, really?' Rochelle looked genuinely puzzled. Like weren't Buddhists from Asia or was it India?

Monica carried on, 'Anyway, I'm promoting a workshop here in town next month, the guru Mahinua is to talk, just wondered if you would be interested. Look, I know Anya you work for a regional TV channel.'

Anya was getting visibly flustered. Her body language was not good. Then the training kicked in. It was not automatic, when you were undercover, she got out a business card from her shoulder bag.

'Look, give me a ring on Monday and we will have a chat, she flung the card on the bar and turned towards Rochelle. 'We have to go.' Beth looked at in curiosity. It said RT correspondent, true. 'Come on Rochelle, let's go.' She looked dazed. They both got up, turned and walked to the door, just like that. Monica watched them go.

She was mystified and Rochelle had also looked puzzled; then had left their drinks unfinished, she had not expected this, was it something she had said? Had she overstepped some mark? She turned around to find Beth's eyes meeting hers.

'What are you up to, Monica?

She replied, 'Trying to make my day job work outside my work I guess.'

Beth frowned. 'Well, don't then!' They turned away from each other. Monica was embarrassed, she had not expected any of this. She was going to ask Beth for the card, but let it go. Get it another time.

Pablo had not heard any of this, he was upstairs in his office. He had been on the Omegaplex's Facebook page, there was a lot of interest out there, there was time for walk-ins, it was not raining, always a plus – hope for northern, small-town nightlife. He was all set to put the pizzas on but he needed trading standards to vet the kitchen before he could offer food to the punters. He would hope to be doing takeaways soon but that was a while away. He wanted to get the flat finished for the kids upstairs first. He would be going on the door himself tonight. Too much to do at the same time.

Yes, he had refused to have an artist called Johnny Hashback at the open mike because it might draw attention to the darker side of the club. Nobody understood the thin white line he had to tread, you didn't shake gossip off easily.

At least, he could always be certain his bands would turn up. This time they had hidden the ganja in the bass drum, that had been exchanged on Friday afternoon upon the moor, long before they got here; the previous time it was in a guitar case. Judd, the saving grace of the operation, was still on board. But for how much longer, he thought.

Then he heard a commotion downstairs. He ran down to the bar. The police dog team had come in. A cold sweat broke out on Pablo's forehead. Were there any under-age drinkers in? Any spliffs alight in the basement?

'We are looking for the landlord – am I speaking to him?' the officer said.

'Yes, Pablo Perez is my name.'

'We have come to do an under-age check in the bar. Can we just inspect ID?' There were two teenage girls in the corner following this with surprise, but he was pretty sure they had been checked by Beth. Certainly, everyone else was well over 25. He had briefed all the bar staff, now including Martin, to check age. 'Ladies, may I see your ID, please?'

They both produced their cards. 'Very good, thank you, goodnight.' They left with their dogs.

Pablo gulped. Why bring sniffer dogs into the pub, if indeed, it was a trawl for underage drinking? It didn't add up. They had not brought them three weeks ago when they first checked here. Now they could have taken dogs downstairs but they hadn't even gone down there. The band was under strict instruction since the fiasco last week, so there was nothing to be found. No, this was intimidation, pure and simple.

All eyes were on him. He needed to make a statement. 'Sorry about that, ladies and gentleman, I'm sure it was just a new routine, we always ask for ID, like anywhere else if you are under 25.' The two girls giggled, they looked to be half-cut already, but the racing correspondent shuffled his paper and got up to leave. He must not allow this to happen again, word would get around.

He could not be certain, but could there have been a leak? Could it be Martin? He hoped not. The downbeat guy who always drank on his own in the corner looked at him over the rim of his glasses. What was his name? Kenneth? No that was the other one, the racing guy. He looked away and spoke to Beth. The couple in the corner exchanged glances. 'I will be on the door for the band tonight, don't worry,' and turned to go.

The front door had opened and a rowing couple came in, the woman in tears; now what! The couple that came in the door when a group of just teenagers having are right barny. 'I met him on Tinder, he is a right bastard,' she blurted.

Beth and Monica frowned. Martin turned away. It was going to be one of those nights and it was going downhill fast. Martin thought he knew why, but he had kept his side of the bargain, he had said nothing. Who then? Who could be held to blame?

The two girls had come up to the bar for another Sambuca. 'Another one, ladies?' Monica said.

'Oh, yes!'

They were getting tipsy; she would have to draw the line after these. The newcomer came to the bar while Monica groped in her handbag. Monica handed her a tissue. She asked, 'What's the problem?'

She replied, 'Isn't he horrible?'

The bloke had already fled. *Wisely*, she thought.

'Who is?' she asked. 'He said his name was Jules.' Realisation dawned, wasn't he the very vain guy on the pimp counter in the gents? Apparently, he had been given the job to prevent the punters sniffing coke in the toilets.

Pablo absorbed it as he walked back to the ticket office. He did remember Jules, he had some side business in the gents, which he had encouraged to discourage drug use on the premises. He would, however, now have to find some excuse to either get rid of Martin or cut him in, but he did not want to do that because he could not then make ends meet. He cursed Judd once again, he could not let him go. He would leave it a month so that nobody would hopefully make that connection, he thought. *This is your mess, sort it out. Get the food offer up and running, one less salary to pay.*

'Tickets, please.' He smiled at his punters, as they descended the stairs. Da Kingston Boys were tuning up. Onwards and somewhere, he reflected. It was filling up again; but would a pizza oven solve his finances? He was in a massive quandary. The northern soul night was next Saturday and that should sell out. There was just a DJ to look after. He would have to bring in security for that. Not every event needed to revolve around drugs, and he had to be honest, wished he had not allowed them in the first place.

Then Monica's sister Kate came in with former boyfriend Paul. Monica took one look and brushed past Pablo down the stairs. She fled into the ladies, where she burst into tears. She swilled her face. What a bad night it had been. She would leave early before it turned ugly. She came up the stairs. She was crestfallen. 'I have to go early,' was all she said. Pablo shook his head, what were these women like?

Chapter 30

Barry, the druid, was talking to Rob. He was a long-standing customer of his veg box business. 'I hear this Buddhist monk is speaking soon in Frackburgh.' Barry was part of a pagan sect and visited Stonehenge at the solstices. He was also a Namastaia subscriber. He had planted a circle of crystals around the town.

Rob said, 'You know, the way we run our economy is damaging our climate, our environment and people themselves.'

'Ah. You mean the invisible hand,' Barry replied.

'It's very interesting. I, for one, am odds-on to go. There is too much anger on the streets, life is bigger than that; this will be a breath of fresh air for Frackburgh.'

Chapter 31

Anya was pleased with the pressure she was putting on the club and had identified Judd as the major dealer in town. The police always attempted to be one step ahead of the criminal, hence, this sting operation. She also had her informer Angus, in Muirside, not a place she would be "seen dead in if she could help it". Yes, she had befriended him at the races, he lived in the 'tower' as it was known. He had recently come out of his prison term on a licence and was in a halfway house.

Although she had failed so far to secure the evidence she needed for a genuine prosecution, she was confident she would get one soon. She needed to catch him red-handed. He was the wholesaler who supplied the lowlife dealers there. She had been frustrated by the switch of rendezvous lately and it looked like both his flat and the club were clean. She had made the link between Jamaica and the bands coming to town. That was all conjecture. Pablo was the key to its origin and he would crack sooner or later or make a mistake if, indeed, he knew what was going on.

Igor had not picked up anything in Judd's flat either. That was a surprise. She would have thought Judd would have stashed the drugs there; she was working undercover with the border police in Dumfries to crack down on drug dealing in the town. It was called "Operation Priam". She was not dealing with fools. She also had her eyes on the traveller's site for other stashes. The warden had rung Dumfries police. He had reported a store cupboard, they were all screwed up 'round the edges. She might get to the bottom of that through Rochelle. Maybe it was that ex-army scrap merchant they had talked about?

Nobody had yet rumbled her RT cover, which allowed her free passage and she had secured her funding for one more year. It was all about concentration and attention to detail; nothing left to chance. One thing that did bother her was what would happen if a real RT reporter turned up, but there did not appear to be one in the north. She was also working with Maya, who was part of her team, photos of the clientele, which she would keep on her database, to correlate with her known dealers on Muirside. Judd was usually on them. This was not in accordance with the data protection act either.

Though it had been the closest of calls tonight when Monica had asked for the publicity, she had panicked and left with Rochelle before they had finished their drinks. Of course, she would have had to go anyway, as she knew the dogs were coming because she had organised that. She did have feelings for Rochelle, she could not deny Rochelle was a pitiful creature who had endured a very poor start in life and despised her own culture. She applied as a streetwise as Rochelle. She could expand her intellect though. She had to appear to fit in. But she also had a job to do.

She would need to invent a reply from RT in response to Monica's request. She would also need to attend the Buddhist workshop next week, courtesy of maintaining her cover. It was something different. There was a small risk that this might go wrong, were Monica to contact the station directly, and not use her mobile number on her fake card. Then her cover-op could be blown. Then there was also the issue of entrapment, in the offer she had made to Judd. She would have to speak to her supervisor at border police.

He was sure to let her off with a verbal warning. Monica was not stupid, she might read between the lines, like a proper journalist herself rather than an actor like herself, constantly checking her every move. But she got a buzz off it.

Chapter 32

The Buddhist vibe was apparent in the room. Small prayer wheels, powered by batteries, rotated on the window sills. Martin scratched his head, he had seen one of these at a local Chinese in town. He sniffed the air, something sweet, had they been burning joss sticks in here as well?

He was in the town hall assembly rooms, somewhere he would normally pass by and definitely outside his comfort zone tonight. He saw Judd and Beth come in. He walked over towards them and they waved. No bar here! The building's arched roof dated back to medieval times, he knew.

A lot of people he knew were here. The Friends of the Earth, the Greenpeace crowd, the pagan, Barry. Clive was already here too, there were full rows of chairs and upfront, a stage with a bookcase-size Buddha sitting on the table. Behind the table were crimson drapes. Was that Monica on the stage? Yes, she was arranging a microphone, dressed in a black kaftan. Was she a Buddhist too, wasn't that something Beth had said? Anya had come in, yes she was a journalist, so it was said.

There was a sudden hush as if everyone there was holding their breath at the same time. Mahinuata came on to the stage. He was barefoot, clad in saffron-yellow robe. To widespread applause. Couldn't he afford shoes? Apparently, not. He hushed the audience with a gesture but there was no need, his presence was sufficient. He addressed them in a very statesmanlike manner. They hung on his every word.

As he settled into his discourse, he rattled phrases off, such as, '...dislocation of species from environment...' '...seventeen layers of spirituality...', 'So today the greatest tragedy is the absence of a sense of the tragedy – fourth century AD,' and then came 'Vegetarianism' and 'respect to animals'. He looked around, there were a few more saffron-yellow robes in the audience too.

Presumably, the saffron robes in the audience belonged to initiates from the monastery. Then it was all over and the Monk said a blessing in a language he did not recognise.

Anya really took in what she was hearing. Monica had asked her earlier whether RT was going to film the event. She had told another lie. She said her camera crew had been called to a road incident. She had her first pangs of conscience when she thought of her role in the war on drugs. She would have made a better journo! Did she overact the part, was she too strident, was she always within the law or just outside it? It was easy to fool Rochelle but Monica? Who was she to play the moral high ground?

After the talk was over, Martin went up to talk to Anya with Clive just behind. Clive was saying, 'What's your own take on this Buddhist idea? What language was he talking in with his blessing? Seems like a lot of self-sacrifices to me.'

'It's all about climbing your own mountain, I guess,' said Anya, 'but I may be wrong, not in an ego way. He is trying.' She paused to think, '…to connect with a wider audience outside his monastery.' She thought further, 'I can identify with his comfort zone.'

Monica came down to chat. A discussion was to follow. 'It was moving,' she said. They all nodded in agreement.

Then Martin said, 'But he doesn't have to live in Frackburgh.' They all laughed. None of them had been to *San-u-delin* either.

Monica said, 'Did you hear that blessing? It was in Parsi.'

Clive asked, 'What language?'

'Apparently nobody uses it now,' Beth said. 'I'm a humanist. I understand his intention. You have got to have some faith, I can't imagine being an atheist.'

'Did you see those two missionaries in the town centre? They would never show their face here! Apparently, they came all the way from America to convert us to their faith, who did they say they were? Yes, Church of the higher-order

'Oh, that god squad! They send some rookie pair of kids over every year. 'They want to walk with you, treat you like morons. Where are they from Salt Lake City? Not even in the same ballpark as this guy. Are they? Oh no…'

Chapter 33

Monica was now working on the next issue. She had eventually persuaded the monastery to take out a box advert and the event had thankfully paid for itself, with donations. It also helped to pay for the journal to go to press the week before. She would now have to spend a few days contacting her advertisers to comply with the new European computer security legislation. The monastery had not been that willing to engage, they were not of this world; they relied on donations themselves, but it was a useful point of contact for the specialist readership of a publication like Namastaia.

She had already asked the editor for a spin-off – an advertorial from Mahinuata. She could not fathom where Anya was coming from, though. She had approached her as a fellow journalist but had been rebuffed in no uncertain way. Why were these Russians so assertive? She had seemed evasive and made promises she did not keep. Why did people keep doing that?

The editor had a chiropody business, which she ran in the mornings and then devoted time to the magazine in the afternoon. Sometimes they did the whole thing on one theme and this next one was to be on Buddhism. It all required a lot of planning.

Frackburgh Housing Action Trust was a community group converting redundant buildings into public housing for local people. She wanted to get involved. There was a balance to be had between ruin and salvation, she mused.

She always enjoyed trawling for business, early doors in the three-monthly cycle the magazine worked on. She was on the phone to the College of Delphic studies in Kensington, an established workshop provider for the high-end London market, Hampstead Heath, where they had more subscribers than the rest of England. They would renew for a whole year of four issues, she was certain. That would bring in £600 over the year. When she got up to £25,000, they would have enough money to go to the press.

Chapter 34

It was the first hands-on day for Rochelle at the call centre at Frackburgh business park. They had not queried anything on her CV, which had surprised her, and after a week learning the ropes, she had been let loose on selling Citroëns. She now found herself in a salesroom, among her cohort and along with sixty experienced hands, a cacophony of competing voices. She was faced with a complex computer programme.

The staff seemed to be even younger than her. They were a transient bunch; staff turnover was enormous. She was looking at herself in the mirror in the toilets on one of her rare quarter of an hour breaks. They all seemed inured to the task.

The computer had a screen to tell her what to say and another window telling how to price spot-items. This had coloured lettering on a black background. She had spent a godly part of the week practising her spiel. If she made a sale then her call would be recorded and assessed by her bosses. How much more stressful could it be?

She had signed up for this, so she would have to grin and bear it. Anya had told her it could work, she trusted her – and it paid weekly. The calls came through on a random loop without warning and she started to read out what it said on the screen. It all had to be worded perfectly and she did not feel up to speed at all.

Some of the callers could be hard work. Was it really true that the owner of 10 Citroëns only went on holiday in Portugal because oil filters were cheaper?

Chapter 35

'Ladies and gentlemen, please welcome Rob.' It was another Tuesday night open mike for Clive and Monica. This second week, he managed, with help from Monica and Martin, to find a drummer, who could accompany any guitarists. The advantages were obvious. A couple of six formers had also shown up, full of enthusiasm, though perhaps not yet as skilled on their instruments.

Rob, (aka Roy) the drummer, was a muscular man who was doing a postgrad, a friend of the cleaner, Martin, apparently. He worked on an organic allotment out by the estuary and ran a veggie box scheme. What was it called? Kelpby? Clive was pleased. Maybe they could find a bass player too? He would ask Rob if he knew of anyone. Scull had returned too, he was going to do some Fairport Convention – "meet me on the ledge". He had told him that he preferred it here to the monthly folk club up at the rugby ground, it had more energy here.

Clive and Monica beamed at each other – it was going well on the whole. It was almost as if he had summoned her when he had suggested the idea. What was it that Mon had said to him? 'You are only doing as well as your last gig you know.' That was it. She was so right. He would invite Louise for the following Saturday here.

On the way out, Pablo asked his advice on the proposed pizza preparation area. Clive had filled out all the paperwork for environmental health, together with a measured plan of the alterations required – a new door opening here, a serving hatch there. Stainless steel never came cheap.

The jury service was playing havoc with Pablo's routine, his contact with his children and he had involved Clive in the planning. It only cost him a few beers now and then. It was taking time to come to terms with.

Chapter 36

It was another mid-week at the club. The Omegaplex kitchen was almost ready for its inspection. Pablo had done a lot of the work himself in the evenings. The stainless steel glistened under the fluorescent lighting. Jury service got in the way, though.

He surveyed his realm. All that glistened was not gold. It had now turned into his prison. The music was the solace, the drugs the grist.

The Northern soul night had passed without incident, the bouncers had seen to that. He had added a karaoke to it, at which both Clive and Monica had sung.

Pablo realised the time had come. He had put it off too long. Martin had to go. He was now running at a loss. He would make him redundant and cite the failing finances of the club as the reason. He sighed. He only had himself to blame. When you are managing change, it isn't easy. He really liked Martin, he would now have to do the cleaning himself, he supposed.

Ramos and Juliana were in residence upstairs, with all the pent-up energy of childhood. They were quite a handful every day. Martin was downstairs, still doing his mid-week cleaning.

He waited for him to come upstairs. He could no longer look him in the eye.

Chapter 37

Rob was on his veg box round and then out to Kelpby to work on the farm. He had to fit it all around his postgrad at Napier University. He lived in Muirside, it was all he could afford. There were few customers on this estate, but it was part of his routine.

There were a few people worth avoiding on this estate. He spotted Jimmy coming out of the bookies. He crossed the road to avoid him. This proved to be the safer option. He had previously complained to the estate office of Manseboro Heart about this dealer on the estate but nothing had happened, it was to no avail. He spotted him crossing to his side of the road, he looked dreadful. He had not even noticed.

Angus, he knew as well. He was in a halfway house, out of prison and dealing on the streets, around the corner from him in Bellingham Tower.

Chapter 38

Rochelle's shift was coming to an end. She was absolutely shattered. The constant droning had grated on her nerves. It was so noisy. It was definitely a diary entry day.

Most calls seemed to be answered by elder couples, they were a hard sell. The computer work was complicated. She had only used a commodore 64 before; she only knew the name of the called when it came up on the screen.

She eventually made a sale; only to be reprimanded by the moderator, who had played what she had said back to her. She had apparently deviated from the script on terms and conditions and the sale was invalidated, he said. She had said something about insurance. She should have called it a plan. With a bonus based on sales, this was an unpromising start for her independence.

She had listened on headphones back to what she had said. Did her voice really sound so shrill? She had to agree it was not a good call. She gulped. 'I will try and get it right next time,' she said. The moderator nodded. She blushed.

What had she let herself in for? She sighed, picked up her coat and left the building. It was too early to know. She was sure her dad would tell her what a fool she was to try and better herself. Still, she would have some money in the bank the following Friday.

Chapter 39

Mr Perez. The usher had approached him. 'Please come with me to Court two.' Pedro was grateful as he had enough of hanging around. He followed him into an imposing panelled room. Barristers with white wigs were moving around. It was all very odd. He was joined by another 10 jurors as they were led to their seats on their side of the court. They milled into place and sat.

Almost straightaway, it was, 'All rise.' The judge had entered the court from behind his throne. It was surreal, like being at church. 'In the case of the Crown v. Teresa Bunting. The charge is drug-dealing.' The judge called, 'Case for the prosecution.' The barrister was touching his waistcoat and addressed the throng. 'I call my first witness. Call Jake Fellowes.'

A shifty looking character shuffled to the witness stand. 'Can you tell the court your name?'

'Jake Fellowes…'

Pedro had come out in a cold sweat, he was no longer listening. This was all too close to call. It could just as easily be him up in the dock.

Chapter 40

Back at the Omegaplex that evening, Pablo had two things on his mind – how to commemorate the thirtieth anniversary of the Specials and getting rid of Martin. The presence of a couple in the corner of the bar, another concern for him in this instance. Pablo wondered – would they be gone before he had the chat? Was it going to work? The couple finished their drinks and left, then Martin came up to the bar. 'Martin, can I have a chat please?'

'OK.' *Uh-oh*, he thought.

'As you know, this club is going through a rough patch – look at this afternoon, only two people in here. So I'm going to have to scale down. I am giving you a month's notice. I will give you a month's wage if you want to leave today.'

Martin was incandescent with rage. *So no respect then?* He thought he had been promoted to the barman. 'Is that so? You have not, repeat, not heard the last of this!'

He walked out of the club before he exchanged a blow with Martin, who shouted, 'Don't forget your P45!'

He thrust it into Martin's hand and left with a slam of the door.

Pablo closed up the club for the day. He was in no mood to serve anyone else tonight. The court case had really rattled him. Returning back to the kids upstairs for an evening meal, he needed to think about what he was going to do that court case! Now he had to carry on regardless. This was where the real fun started.

Chapter 41

Anya was being quizzed by her boss at Border police in Dumfries. Detective superintendent Piper was the silver Chief Inspector for "Operation Priam". His office was a murky green with a frayed brown carpet-tiled floor. It had not seen a lick of paint in years. The meeting was not going well, however.

'I'm glad you have come to see me, Anya.' After some uncharacteristic hesitation, he continued. 'The crime wave in the borders is, we are pretty certain, being fed by drug takers, but your Russian gangster routine is probably unlawful, unprofessional and frankly, not a credible entrapment. You must not instigate agent provocateur and entice another to commit an express breach of the law, which they would not otherwise have committed and then proceed to inform against them in respect of such an offence.

She looked down at her hands and re-joined, 'It's not easy, you know, to play this role. I never told him I worked for RT. You have to think on your feet, I want him to make a mistake and I need to spook him.'

'Stick to your RT identity in the future. Otherwise, your overconfidence and risk-taking will undo you. If people question your legends, you will be revealed.' She retaliated, 'It's not as if I am sleeping with him, is it?'

Her boss laughed, 'But what would you have done if he had accepted that you're supposed to be a London money launder? Careful, Anya.' He added, 'You don't know, do you?'

Anya replied, 'I would have asked for a budget to lend me the money!'

'You are joking!' He shook his head. 'There is no need to be flippant, Anya. We are cut to the bone already. Luckily for you, I trust your intuition, but you need to clear this sort of thing with me in advance, so we can avoid its repetition in the future. At least you have got that husky to protect you and he gets his food allowance. OK, you may go.'

She glared at him and said, 'Thank you, sir.' She walked straight back out of the door; she had left Igor in the car.

She left HQ, disgusted with herself. *Thanks for nothing*, she thought. Was there an element of sexism at work here? He was not at the sharp end. It was not all about climbing the greasy pole, was it? At least she had Igor. She opened her car door, looked in his eyes. Their eyes were the same colour; he was always pleased to see her. He was good at sniffing for drugs as well. A policewoman's job is not a happy one. She had to remember she was ruled in every respect by the law of the land.

She would ring Rochelle; they should have some fun tomorrow. She would take her to the new LGBT club, what was it called, Reynards? She might let slip some lead, you never know, and would no doubt have some interesting snippets of life in a call centre! She chuckled and started the engine.

Chapter 42

Martin was pacing up and down the flat. He was still seething. He had accepted a month's wage in lieu of working his notice. And a P45. He would still make an anonymous phone call to the police, he ought to use a phone box, it would be harder to trace and he could scarper as soon as he had got through.

He had heard of crime stoppers but he did not know the number, so would use 101. Pablo had made a big mistake, deliberate, cruel and his last, he hoped. He had rung up his mate, Rob from the farm, who had advised him to contact the police.

'I do play the drums there, you know, mate,' he had said. 'I cannot believe they would stoop this low. I hope I am wrong. We do have a massive problem on the estate, true.'

He needed to speak to his girlfriend Rita. What would she think? Would she support him? Was it sensible? All in the right order, he thought to himself. He got his mobile and dialled her. 'Listen, I got to do something brave today.' He paused, 'I need to make a call. I will come and see you and stop over tomorrow.'

Chapter 43

Reynards had previously been a humble café. You would have difficulty in guessing that looking at it now. A posy of flowers framed the logo above the door. This was no florists, though; it was the only burlesque bar in town. There was never any trouble here. No kiddie fiddlers anywhere.

Anya frowned. Her plan to tie Rochelle up at the call centre had given her time to case the traveller site without drawing suspicion. Gypsies and travellers had their own site in Frackburgh and were council tenants.

She had posed as a debt collector. The boss would have reprimanded her. Luckily, the warden was not around; he might have asked for ID, which would have been awkward. She certainly could not have made her RT journo role work here. No more Russian gangster. Her kudos had already been questioned by Monica. She needed to show she could get results.

She had not gone down well on-site; the hostility of travellers was palpable. What was the point of going further? There was no sign of the scrap metal van she had been looking for either. Nor this guy Jimmy, he didn't live here was all they would say. Of course, she didn't have to believe that.

She believed, he was either a fence for stolen goods or a dealer. A lot of what went on here, she believed, was unchallenged and unpunished. She needed to identify the driver and track the licence plate, but it would only raise suspicions if she asked Rochelle. Once she had that, she could use the automatic number-plate-recognition system to track the vehicle and its owner's address. Where did he even live? Not here. They had closed ranks, said they had not seen him for weeks. He was sure to be somewhere in the vicinity, she was convinced.

She had arrived before Rochelle and hoped she would fit in here. She walked through the doors and took it all in. It was very different from the Omegaplex. She found a chair; she straightened out her legs and hips. The venue had only opened the previous month. She had been meaning to check it out before. There was a red rocking horse next to the stage with a tinsel backdrop. But maybe it was a unicorn? It had only one horn. Bizarre. There was some sort of drag cabaret planned tonight, so it said on a poster. She went up to the bar and noticed Jules behind. She had seen him before somewhere – was it from the Omegaplex?

She opened her bag. She looked down on the floor, there appeared to be dropped coins, but when she aimed a kick at one, she realised it must have been glued to the floor. Why? She was all in favour of open-mindedness, this just seemed duplicitous…

At that moment, Rochelle strolled in. They exchanged hugs with each other. 'There are some weird people in here,' Rochelle said. They laughed.

'It is quite exciting, though,' replied Anya. Rochelle smiled. There were so many bars they could go to.

The cabaret had started. It was startling. Striking. Burlesque, definitely. It was all a bit overdone, it reminded her of "Versailles" on TV. Anya did not know what to think, but Jules was there in full drag. Anya quizzed her, 'How is the job going?'

Rochelle pulled a face. 'Not well. It is far more difficult than I had been led to believe in the job shop. I don't have any of the computer skills, the experience or anything else I need.' Rochelle looked flustered.

'You have the gift of the gab though, don't you? Are you going to carry on with it?'

Rochelle considered. 'I need to give it time; it is far too early to know.'

'How much time?'

Rochelle thought and replied, 'Three months. Thanks for pointing me that way, even if I am not enjoying it.'

Anya replied, 'You deserve that support, Rochelle. I didn't get to be an RT reporter by sitting on my backside, you know. Women have paid the highest cost, with their bodies, their work and their lives.'

'You might be interested to know then, Anya that on the Friday before Christmas, it is a tradition in this town for the men in this town to go out and have a punch up! We call it black-eyed Friday...' Anya pretended to look shocked.

'Really? I am sure they never have that problem here at Reynards.'

Of course, she knew about that, she was police through and through; it was their busiest night of the year, bar New Year's Eve. Anya looked around for the toilets. She needed a pee. 'Back in a mo,' she said. There was only one, a unisex, just like she had seen in Paris. The symbol on the door was ambiguous – half trouser, half skirt. She got it – transgender.

When she had gone, Rochelle wondered yet again. What is going on here? Was it a seduction? She sighed, it must be a come on. She followed the route Anya had taken to the toilets. They had agreed they would keep in touch.

Chapter 44

Martin was in the bath with his girlfriend Rita. It was the next morning following his call to the police. Her sleepy, brown eyes met with his, framed by soapsuds. 'You know, darling, I would rather be a lover than a coward. You know that,' he said. He absorbed the sight of her.

She smiled, 'You contacted the police, then, darling?'

The most gorgeous woman he had ever been with.

'Yes, I did what I said I would. The meek are forced to fight for the right to life. First, I went and got the pay-off money and my P45 off Pablo. That put me in a bad mood, oh, yes. Then I rang 101 from the nearest phone box, it took a minute to get through, left the details and then ran off and moved on as quickly as I could. I don't care what happens to the Omegaplex anymore. Pablo did not stick by his side of the bargain. He needed to be stopped.' He would make sure of that.

'Take care, lover.' She looked serious. 'Don't put yourself in any danger.'

He re-joined, 'Well, how would they know it was me? I can't think how. Everything to lose.'

She frowned. 'I hope you are right. What is best for the powerful is not best for the powerless. Don't slip up, you stay close to me.'

He grinned. 'I certainly will, I am now!'

She was a friend for life. It was all like a dream, like candlelight on strands of hair.

Chapter 45

'They will quiz you about where you see the company in five, ten or fifteen years and what key challenges you expect the ALMO to face in that time.' Clive was thinking of becoming a non-executive director of a local social housing organisation. It was being run into the ground at present.

He was on the phone in discussion with a non-exec recruitment agency he had found on the internet. It was a new business model, apparently, and they were keen to hire. Monica had prompted him to get involved, she was a kind person. The voice continued, 'How you answer interview questions will reveal your approach to strategic considerations and whether you can provide solutions for potential flaws in the current business model.'

'I hear what you say,' Clive replied.

The voice continued, 'This will be your opportunity to turn the tables. Ask them, as an architect, what challenges they face and what expertise they are specifically looking for.'

Clive was hooked. The call was to put his name forward to the newly formed Frackburgh housing trust; they wanted him to become a non-executive director. Monica had put him on to this. He beamed.

He had green credentials to uphold. He was naturally a creative person. 'I believe I have a lot to offer,' he replied. 'The local housing set-up is not working – it's an ALMO called Muirsebro Heart, they just sit on the housing problem and fail to deal with problem tenants and discriminate against the poor. They even used Bellingham Tower as a halfway house.' Time, he thought, to move beyond biscuits and tyres! His dad would approve.

'They also need to be more eco-conscious.' He could advise on that. We need to mobilise a carbon army of workers to retrofit and insulate homes. The ball was in his court. Thirty years ago, environmentalist policies were intended to prevent us from running out of fossil fuels. Now it's a case of having too much fossil fuel for the environment to handle.

Chapter 46

'There has been a tip-off,' Anya's silver handler was addressing her in his office, at Dumfries police station.

'Unfortunately,' he continued, 'the caller rang off before we could get any details or trace the number.' He was saying. Anya was excited. She listened intently to her boss.

'Was it about the club, sir?

He continued, 'Yes, Anya, you were right, whoever it was, rang our 101 line, but we did get a recording though, as normal.'

Anya paused. 'I might recognise the voice,' she said.

'I have it here.' Her boss played the recording. She listened; the voice was familiar. 'Sir, I think it is the cleaner, his name is Martin.'

Her boss smiled, 'How are we going to proceed, Anya?' We do have a budget to work within, as you know.'

'They are canny operators, the drugs are being stored off-site somewhere and maybe are not usually in the club in the first place, they were sloppy that day, I had your dog team in but I haven't yet found where, I also employed Igor on Judd's flat, an absolute zero. If I were to approach Martin, he might well clam up, and it would blow my cover. I was so disappointed with Judd but sir, I did realise I overplayed my hand. This is why I came to see you. I do have an informant on the estate, a guy called Angus, but he did not know the dealer. He has only just come out of prison, so he knows quite a bit of lowlife.'

'There has to be a solution, Anya, I am not putting you down, you have produced a credible lead scenario. Gold is impressed. We have invested so much time and money already and we are so close this time. The gold command is adamant that these addicts are causing a crime wave throughout the borders; they will stop at nothing to buy their next fix. No doubt without it, they might turn to opioid addiction, but we can only deal with one issue at a time. Anya, we must have a conviction!' With that, the sergeant reflected on his brother, who became addicted to the drug oxycontin and had subsequently lost his job. There was a pause.

'Indeed, sir. I need to trace a man called Jimmie, I believe he may live on Muirside, the danger here is we end up shopping that particular street dealer but the big fish has slipped the net. I suspect Judd might be using him as the go-between.'

'You need firm evidence of such a link, Anya; this is not watertight at all. We cannot just arrest people on hearsay, we need a red-handed capture and we need it soon.'

'I am aware of that, sir. Let me find a way, I need at least a week to build the case.'

Chapter 47

Anya had been thinking. All these months in the field she had been on permanent overtime and frankly, she would be bored out of her skull were she to return back to Dumfries HQ for a desk job. She got a buzz out of it. She was a trained problem solver. Could she pull it off?

The next day, she drove to Muirside. She was on a fishing expedition, looking for Jimmie the scrap metal van man. She had covert photos of most of the punters entering the club but he never seemed to be one of them. She had printed out the photos from her memory stick. She had pinned them up, incident room style, in her office flat. Did he leave his van in a lock-up? She had already checked the electoral role but there was no Judd on that. She felt uncomfortable on the estate but decided to go into the bookies. Might he be a regular gambler like herself?

She went into the betting office. Eyes swivelled around as she walked in, she stood out like a sore thumb. She was the only woman in here for one thing. She realised she had made a big mistake, wearing her leather pants and a white blouse. She should have dressed down today, maybe a grey shell suit, hoodie-like, no makeup. Maybe she should have asked Rochelle where Jimmy lived, but what possible excuse could she have used?

She turned around and left. This was going nowhere and then some. When she visited Angus, she had never made the mistake she had today. Still, Jimmie might be on the housing association register; might indeed even be getting housing benefits. She was in deep thought as she got into her car.

At that moment, she looked up and glimpsed Judd on the opposite side of the road and – a stroke of luck if ever there was one – he was talking to someone else. They had not seen her, so she quickly drove off and circled the block. Where were they headed? Could it be Jimmy? She had now driven up behind them. She slowed down and waited turning off the engine. If they looked behind them, all would be lost. They were headed for the tall tower block, Bellingham Tower.

If she followed, Judd would certainly recognise her. Not worth the risk of arousing suspicion at any cost. Enough for one day, she thought, most likely this is where Jimmy lives. It was time to follow this up through the back-office enquiries. She rang her boss in Dumfries.

'I am in Muirside, sir. I think our fence Jimmy lives in Bellingham Tower; I have seen him with Judd walking that way. Could we ask housing benefit if they have a claimant of that name in that block? Sorry, I don't know the surname.' She waited for his reply. 'Thanks, sir.'

The next stage was more difficult, she could not organise a search warrant without due cause and merely seizing the stash, if it was here, would be pointless unless it could be traced back to the club. Was that likely? She thought, could it be some grudge match; might it even be a rival drug dealer? Couldn't it be?

She wondered if she could now persuade Martin to give evidence. It was a calculated risk with a disadvantage. It only implicated the club in so far as Judd's swag was found there. Could she use her supposed female intuition and the RT front to get him to volunteer that she had one over him?

She had no better ideas. The cover was coming to an end, anyway. She made the call to her silver Chief Inspector. Maybe he might talk to her? She got through to her boss. 'Sir, my role is done. We risk it all on the grievance, I reveal my role, I know the caller and we see what happens.' There was a long silence.

'Anya, I would agree, but a stake-out at Bellingham Tower might be more productive, because if you are right, that is where the swag will be going, and we need a legal catch with the goods. Your customary persistence could pay off. Get back to me, the budget is best spent on that now.

Even if it fails, we can pick up this low life scum in Muirside so do some good? Do not fail me, Anya!'

Chapter 48

She drove back into town and parked near the club. She went into the Omegaplex. It was of an evening sunset, a gloaming mid-week. The leaves on the trees had turned russet. Leaf fall was beginning to clog up the roads and pavements. She was waiting for the housing information on Jimmy, but in the meantime, needed to find out where Martin was, he was after all a cleaner here. She had to feel the vibe and latch on to it.

As usual, Pablo was at the bar. How was she going to handle this? Well, act like any other punter, start by ordering a drink. 'Vodka and tonic, please. There was no other staff around, in fact, any clientele at all. 'Quiet today, then.' Pablo frowned, what was this woman after? There was no need to draw attention to the fact that there were only the two of them here, was there?

'Well, the girls only come in on Fridays and Saturdays,' he said.

'Oh, I thought you had another bloke, wasn't it, Martin?'

He looked uncomfortable. 'He no longer works here, Anya. Yes, we did have more staff on when "Da Kingston Boys" were here. Two's enough for most events, anyway.' She was too late then, again. It was time for an exit strategy.

'I was hoping to meet a friend in here, but she doesn't seem to have turned up.' She made a play of fingering her phone. She looked at her watch, I'll give her another five minutes, I think.' That gave her time to finish her drink. She had been reduced to small talk.

'I really enjoy the live music here.'

'Yes,' he replied. 'It is true the club has come on leaps and bounds since I took it over two years ago when it was just a working men's club.'

'Are you still getting those Jamaican bands over?' Pablo was starting to think this small talk was something fishy, but it was probably coincidental…

'Well, yes, I'm on the circuit now,' he replied. She looked at him with those deep blue eyes. 'Really?' Was she taking the piss? 'Yes. They use the Omegaplex as a stepping stone on the way to England.'

She drank up saying, 'Nice work, got to go thanks,' and picked up her bag and walked out of the door. She cursed herself, was he on to her? She hoped not. Could she have done things differently?

Pablo locked up and went down to clean the toilets. Whatever. She was a striking woman, but there was another less endearing quality lurking just below the surface, one best avoided, definitely, he thought. It was called the cold-blooded ruthlessness.

There again, he could have asked her to promote his club on RT. He did not, however, feel confident to broach that. He would instead have to speak to Judd; he knew more about her than he did. He took out his mobile and dialled.

Chapter 49

Clive was talking to Monica, 'I reckon, with all the students coming back for the autumn term, we could pull-off a charity gig.'

Monica asked, 'Yes, I would be up for that. What charity would you have in mind?'

'Well, NASUWT are promoting Rock against Racism. That started after a racist rant by Eric Clapton.' I have checked with them and apparently, they will pay for 5000 flyers. We get one side for the promo, they get the other.'

'I will check with Pablo whether we could do it on a Friday!' he beamed. 'That would be Halloween,' he continued. 'Pablo is not doing his thing until Saturday.'

'I believe it's our commitment to finding where the common good lies.'

He nodded. 'Yes, I will knock up a design in Photoshop.'

Chapter 50

Beth was out shopping in the town centre. She was surprised to notice Martin drinking a coffee at Beanz for Us, in the town square. She had her darling in the pram with her. She sat down at his table. 'Martin? What happened? I thought you had been promoted?'

'No, the opposite, I was made redundant,'

She pondered, 'Why?'

'It's a long story,' he replied.

'I am listening.' Martin sighed. 'What it is that I caught Judd with a large quantity of skunk. I think it must be coming over from Jamaica. There in that club.'

'Really? What did Pablo say about that?'

'He knows, Beth, he is in on this deal!'

She was thunderstruck, this would never have occurred to her. 'You're kidding! Have you thought of stopping him? There had to be some way to sort it out.' *I need support to process this news*, she thought.

'I did ring the police, the balls in their court now. It was anonymous, so I am hoping not to be implicated.' He looked into her eyes. 'It could turn nasty, after all.' She took his hands in hers and said, 'Thank you for sharing that with me, Martin. This cannot be easy for you.'

'Nobody wants to live a lie, Beth. But it seems some people, and Pablo is one, Judd another, have lost all touch with morality, when there is money involved. They are not exactly paragons of virtue. Young people still struggle to make sense of their lives. There are a number of ways you can channel that and music remains one of them. But what is their excuse? The fish rots from the head.' He rubbed his fingers together.

'Who else knows, Martin?'

He reflected. 'Just you and my girlfriend, at the moment.'

She winced. 'Well, if the police won't act, there is always RT. Don't forget Anya would lap this up, a real local story.'

Martin was startled, he had never considered that. 'I will give it a week,' he replied. 'The cops need time to do their best, I will bide my time until then.'

She took a card out of her bag. 'I still have her card...Monica gave it to me after her spat with Anya. So if you want to ring Anya, when you make your mind up, you are welcome.'

She handed it over. 'I suppose I need to be looking for another evening job then,' she said.

Martin nodded, 'I'm sorry, Beth, this has come as a shock to you, as much as it has to me.'

No, just typical of this town, she thought. She sighed. She was a big girl, she could handle it. 'I understand.' There didn't seem any point in it at all.

Chapter 51

Anya had gone to the races. She came here when she needed to think; get away from the acting, maybe work out the odds. She was partial to a little flutter, as Judd knew; it was part of her act. Whatever. She now had an address – Jimmie Alexander, tenth floor, 109, Bellingham Tower.

She also had the registration number of his van and was awaiting the results of its movements over the last two years. Some of them must connect with Judd, surely? There were 3,500 cameras all over the country tracking every single UK vehicle, but only one in this town, at a filling station. Would that be any help? If nothing new came to light, she was going to have to start all over again.

She looked up. Take one step at a time, Maybe Jimmie would be here, he must get rid of his money somewhere. Was he a gambler too? She now had a photo from his army records.

"Operation Priam" was on track again. She was on the prowl with the full support of the law. It was only a question of time before she caught Judd with the gear for Jimmy, surely; but if she could follow it back up the chain, that would be perfect. It must surely come over on the club weekends and she would have another officer on surveillance that Saturday at Bellingham. She had to psyche herself up for the week ahead.

On the other side of the track sat Jimmie. Anya was closer than she knew, but they were in different stands. Nor had she spotted his white scrap metal van in the car park either. He was here because he had sold all the stash and awaited a fresh delivery on Saturday. The major cut of which went back to Judd.

Carrimore had not won after all, but then he was a 40-1 rookie outsider, so he had only lost a fiver, not much really. Kenneth had been wrong, this time; but if he had been right, he would be £200 up.

A large dog indeed! He looked over the course. He liked to come here when the week's business was done. The scrap metal was a good cover for his drops to punters. It was a quiet afternoon, one race done, three to go. As with so many things, he needed to experiment to see what worked and what didn't.

Chapter 52

Judd was on the phone with Pablo. He had missed the previous call. 'So you are saying you sacked Martin? Pablo, he can shop us, I thought you might have bought him off. Anya already suspects me.'

Pablo was aghast. 'Why did you not think to tell me about Anya?'

No clear or easy solution occurred to him. Judd responded, 'Because she has no proof, after all, I don't keep the drugs in my flat. She came around making out like some Russian mafia, with her sniffer dog, it was hilarious. I couldn't see what difference it made.'

Pablo replied, 'She came in the bar too, sniffing around here, actually. I told you she works for RT, the TV channel.' Pablo was furious that he had withheld all this from him. 'You have put our whole future in peril.'

Judd was unrepentant. 'Pablo, you yourself have made an enemy of Martin. If he thinks to speak out, you have brought it on yourself. The more people know, the shakier this set-up looks. OK, I may have misjudged Anya, granted, she is most likely a fraud.

'How is it you thought you could do the exchange in the club anyway? The structure is solid, that is why I told Jimmy never to set foot in your club and you have never met him.' He paused. 'They have yet to make that link. The next shipment is Saturday?'

'"Dubtown International" is coming, yes. We do the drop up in the borders Saturday pm; you take it straight to Jimmie. Let's hope they never make the connection with a scrap metal dealer.'

'Let's hope so, Pablo. We are going to need all the luck we can get.' He had made a mistake with Martin, but it seemed he might get away with it at the time, but he should have checked with Judd first. It was because he could not trust his temper.

Now he himself had endured this visit from Anya, he could see it in another light. It was a colossal error of judgement to make two mistakes in one week.

Chapter 53

Clive had bought two tickets for "Dubtown International" that Saturday morning on the internet – one for himself, one for Louise. For her part, she wanted to find out what all this fuss about two-tone music was. His step-mum had agreed she could stay over his place after the gig, as they didn't want to be woken up in the small hours.

Music was the best thing that happened in this town and while his job was better than most, it was very nitpicking. The best thing about it was to see the buildings complete and know you had helped to make it happen. It was the same with music for him, he was certain. Songwriters and composers also.

The jeep was once again on its way up to the moorland, on the track up to the boggy mire, which formed the Scottish border towards Newcastleton. Judd made the rendezvous call on an unregistered mobile. Pablo caught sight of a car in the distance. The rendezvous was in the same place, around the corner from the Pele Tower, as last time. No CCTV up here, no anything really. They pulled up alongside with a scrunch of tyres. The band had come up in their van, travelling south, from their Newcastleton B and B. Pablo opened the passenger door. Shook the outstretched hand. 'No picnic today, then?'

Sylvester replied, 'No, we got through customs OK, got the budget flight to Edinburgh, it was a doddle. We always seal the bags, so the dogs cannot pick it up. Your generation is finally compensating us, treating the West Indies as crap.'

He yelled with fury, 'We're not immune to that you know, we had to deal with you and all. You have the faith, you know the score, you are now a true Rastafarian.'

Then he grinned, 'Now we have something you want.'
The deal was done.

Chapter 54

The track led down to a clump of trees. Beth and Clive were out in the Lake District, a mere thirty miles away. 'It is good to get away from the town,' she said as they walked along. The woods and trees thickened, the stream dropped into a wood-darkened valley and then they made their way uphill on the far side to the rolling slopes of the tree line, with uncultivated sheep pasture beyond. It had been a glorious day but it showed signs of turning, a storm brewing. A beam of sunlight struck his face.

'Yes,' he replied, 'it is. We are lucky that Denise was able to look after Marilyn today.' She shivered beneath her houndstooth coat. The wind was distinctly nippy, near the top of the ridge. The view was fantastic but only because it was not misty or raining.

'I'm a city boy at heart and find the country seem so empty. Did I tell you, Monica and I are trying to organise a charity gig?'

'Really? That would be really good. We are lucky to have a venue like the Omegaplex, you know. It is a great place to escape here from dictatorship,' she paused. 'I am lucky to have met you, too. I am pleased that I have told you how I felt. We have to find the middle ground and try to cover that as well as we can.' He held her hand. He was glad they had made up. 'Everything in nature has a pattern. I have tried to become aware of the discrepancies between my actions and beliefs. Like saying things because someone else taught you to.'

Suddenly there was silence, peace, and he saw his own life in all its perspective, for once. The four virtues: temperance, wisdom, courage and justice.

Chapter 55

'I am going to drop you and the gear at your gaffe. I don't want to be seen with this vehicle in Muirside.' Pablo was driving back with Judd from the country in the jeep. Judd nodded.

'Pedro, what if my flat is under surveillance?' Pablo turned towards him, eyed him up.

'Don't be silly, the police are too short-staffed for that. You make the final leg of the journey and re-stock Jimmie tout de suite. You will be asking for a bodyguard soon, will you?'

He laughed. Well, that made sense, the jeep with its whip antenna was far too distinctive and easily identified. He had the key to the back entrance of Bellingham Tower, which Jimmie had stolen from its cleaner. He would arrive by bus.

They reached the edge of the town. Not far to go now. He would put it in his rucksack and get the bus down to Muirside, mingle with the crowd. They reached the cul-de-sac where he lived. It was all clear and getting dark.

Back in Muirside, Anya was at the stakeout and the clock was now ticking. She had PC Carol Wren with her and a very large flask of coffee. Drinking it had made her feel headier than ever. Their unmarked car was inauspiciously parked overlooking the entrance to the tower. Two people loitering in a car. It was going to be a long day. Would this fix everything? If only there was a CCTV on that door, but there was not. At some point, the deal would be done. But it could never be certain. This uncertainty was beginning to prey on her brain. In addition, the weather was deteriorating. The day was darkening and it had started to rain. It was true she had been giving training but it was a big ask; for any human being.

It was indeed a long day. When the deal was done, they would nearly miss it all. Anya fiddled with her cup and exchanged glances with Carol. The thermos was running low, she was buzzing with the all that caffeine. It couldn't be long now, surely?

There was only one way in and out. Or so she thought. She had already tried the trades' back door and it was locked. Although they were just the two of them, they would radio for back-up when the time was right. There was a whole team on standby; if it turned up in time. She looked at her watch – 6.30. She sighed.

Back in town, Beth had just put Marilyn to bed. She picked up her mobile. She had decided to contact Anya. It was time to warn her that the police were circling. After all, she was a journalist, wasn't she? RT, she had said. It rang three times before it was picked up.

'Who is this?' a voice she recognised said.

'Anya, its Beth…from the club…you talked to me behind the bar?' Her heart lurched. The voice did seem familiar – Monica's friend. It continued, 'I have some information, an exclusive.'

Oh dear, would she give herself away? 'What sort of information?'

There was a pause. 'The Omegaplex is involved with drug dealing, apparently. We had a cleaner called Martin, who until recently worked there. He caught one of our punters with a large sack of skunk in the toilets. He has tipped off the police after being sacked by the owner. I didn't know anything about it but I wonder if we could meet and have a chat.'

Anya stalled. She might have an arrest by tomorrow but she might not. Who else was in the know? She could not break off from her sortie now, could she? She looked at her watch – 6:30 pm. 'I'm not actually in town at the moment (she lied) but yes, that certainly is of interest to our viewers, it may need a bit more work though. Could we meet somewhere like a coffee shop, say, tomorrow? I know it is Sunday, maybe after lunch?'

Beth agreed to meet her at Beanz for Us on Sunday afternoon in the square at 3 pm. She would have to take little Marilyn with her, she doubted she could get a babysitter at such short notice. She hoped the weather would stay fine. The call was over. She decided to ring Clive to tell him about it.

Back in Muirside, Anya turned to Carol and said, 'I hope that won't be needed.' She bit her lip and continued the sortie. 'We may lose our tactical advantage if there has been a leak.' Just how many people knew? There were comings and goings but no Judd. Where was he?

The bus drew up at the nearby terminus and Judd strolled out, picking up his rucksack from the rack. He was minutes away from the tower. He looked at his watch. 7 pm. Unbeknown to him, Martin was also there, in an adjacent stand, coming off a bus in the opposite direction. He then saw Judd and his rucksack. It looked familiar. On a whim, he decided to follow him, at a distance on the far side of the road.

Martin had reached the Bellingham Tower; Judd was some way in front. He could see him cutting across the grass and looking to be heading for a back entrance. He seemed to be reaching out for his keys; he was getting in that way. Did he really want to get involved? Curiosity had got the better of him. Martin rounded the front corner of the block, the wind whistling around the tower. He made for the front door. At that moment, he came into Anya's field of view. She spotted him.

'Carol, I know that guy from the club.'

Carol replied, 'Perhaps he is after a fix. Ma'am, what is his name?'

'It is Martin – I was expecting Judd rather than him.' Anya furrowed her brows…had she missed something? She decided to check the recky. 'Carol. Keep an eye open, I'm going to see what he has to say about this.' Martin had entered the lobby; he saw the lift was on its way to the top, presumably with Judd in it. He would ring the police again he decided. He dialled 101, the number and waited. At that moment, Anya came through the entrance. He dropped his phone in surprise. She looked at him searchingly.

'Fancy meeting you here,' she offered.

Martin stammered, 'I was following someone, I admit.'

Anya asked, 'Are you an addict, Martin, or a stalker, perhaps?'

He looked shocked, he was shaking his head and this woman was a reporter, wasn't she? There was silence. 'Look, I hear you are a journalist. I rang the police, there is a drugs den up there, its somewhere on the top floor and the supplier with the rucksack is going there.'

Anya acted puzzled. 'He is? Where is he then?'

'He had a key, came in that way.' He pointed to the door behind her. Anya picked up her mobile right away. 'Carol, alpha Priam zero alpha.' This was a scramble code.

'You are no reporter at all, are you?' Martin glared at her.

Anya looked him in the eye, 'Very observant, Martin – I am with Dumfries police.'

'I recognised your voice from your last 101 call, Martin.'

He stammered, 'But I rang off, you can't know it was me.'

She shook her head and simply said, 'You may not realise, but it was recorded, Martin, all 101 calls are, and we are now staking this place out.'

Now Martin was shell-shocked. It really had not been his best idea to come here. It was all because of that stupid rucksack and his hatred for Judd. He should have rung crime stoppers, not the police. He needed time to think, so decided to ask for ID.

Chapter 56

Denise was on the phone to Pablo. It rang and rang. It had been like this for some time, since Pablo had started jury service. She had to pick up Ramos and Juliana after her shift at the hospital.

Pablo sounded flustered when he did pick up. 'Sorry, I took so long to answer, the band are just setting up on stage.'

Denise was curt, 'I will be there in fifteen minutes, so have them all ready to go.'

He replied, 'The kids have been no problem; they find endless fascination with the musicians and all their equipment.'

She smiled. 'Good.' She looked at her watch. 7 pm. She would be there as quick as she could. She had the food ready to go in the fridge when she got back.

She pulled up at the club. Cabs were cruising the street like vultures. The punters were spilling out on to the pavement and as she went in, she saw Monica was behind the bar. They embraced. She went up the stairs, the kids were waiting.

'Mummy!' Juliana was ecstatic. Ramos pulled a face. He had been playing Fortnite with his friends on the internet and didn't want to be pulled away.

She turned around. 'Let's go people.'

Clive had also come in with a woman she did not recognise, she noticed. He was talking to Monica. She waved and let her tribe down the stairs. She wished she could be more enthusiastic about Pablo, though.

Clive was explaining to Monica that Louise had never seen a real reggae band, only UB40. She laughed. 'What's so fake about UB40?'

Clive laughed. 'You know what I mean! Nor are "Dubtown International" Jamaican, they are from Italy.'

Louise said, 'Well, I live in Birmingham, in Aston, where Eddie Grant comes from Electric Avenue. Everybody assumes he lived in Jamaica,' she laughed. ''Round the corner from me.' Monica changed the subject. 'So you are his mum's daughter?'

Louise nodded. 'Yes, Clive is like the cousin I never had.' More laughter. Beth, serving behind the bar, just shook her head. It would be painful if this venue was to die.

Clive said, 'I hope Louise will love it up here.'

Chapter 57

Martin looked over her warrant card. It looked genuine. Then again who could trust ID these days? She looked him in the eye. 'How long ago was it since you came in?'

He parried, 'You really are…er, no more than five minutes actually.'

She said, 'Listen, Martin, it is going to get really busy 'round here in about five minutes. I don't believe you are implicated in all this. You need to speak to my colleague in the car outside and give her your details. We can be in touch later on. You see the silver Ford Focus; well, that's PC Carol Wren in there. Now leave here as soon as you like.'

She looked at the lobby, there could be any number of people getting caught up in the sting, coming and going. She spoke quickly on her mobile. 'Carol, take a statement from Martin, he is already walking towards you. Then drop him at wherever he needs to go, off this estate if possible. How long till they get here? Three minutes, good.' The drug squad were on the way. Half would go in the lift, half up the stairs, leaving her in the lobby. The adrenaline was catching up with her, she needed to prepare herself.

She pressed the lift call button, which showed it to be on the top floor. How long did it take to travel the ten floors? She started the stopwatch on her phone and pressed the call button. At least the lift was working. If the operation went wrong, the suspects would go for the stairs and be met by the squad coming up. There were only the two ways down; the stairs would take much longer than the lift. She counted the seconds. Sixteen, seventeen…and ping! It had arrived. It could be slower. There was a squeal of tyres outside and doors being slammed. She turned around and showed the hit squad the lift. 'Room 109.' They could have been quieter!

Five went in the lift, two up the stairs. The cops had bundled into the lift and shouldered the stair door almost off its hinges. She needed to leave as she wasn't in uniform. Then she wished she was in uniform instead of her usual leather jeans. She rang a number. 'Carol, come and pick me up.' Operation Priam was as good as done.

She waited to see if there was any activity on the stairs for three minutes, but it was blissfully quiet. She walked out the front and saw a rucksack out of the corner of her eye hurtling out of a top floor window. They were jettisoning the evidence! She picked up what was left of it. There were bags everywhere on the grass. Where was Carol? She wished she had not told her to drop Martin off. She dialled the number again. 'Need you here, PC Wren,' she said. On the tenth floor, Room 109 had a steel door and had been opened when the squad reached the corridor. A face had peered out, just a voice, and then it had been slammed shut. 'Police...open up.' The battering ram was slammed into the centre of the door, but it had only made a small dent in the steel sheet. The frame was holding. They would have to drill out the lock. It was all going to take time. Residents were gawping in the corridor at the ferocious onslaught. Nobody came out.

Anya's phone sprung into life. It was Carol returning her call. 'Get the forensics team here now, Carol. It's raining drugs.' She was buzzing with adrenaline.

It was then she had a moment of madness. She rang the real RT hotline and gave them the story. She was a proper reporter now but just pretended to be someone passing the flats, seeing the drugs squad cars, the crime scene set-up and the bags scattered over the grass. This would be the beginning of the end.

It would be the last time she would need to keep up the pretence. She would be re-assigned to somewhere far away like Stranraer, not round here, she was sure.

Chapter 58

Clive was chatting to Monica behind the bar. They were talking about how life had changed since they were kids. 'How come everyone needs a calculator to do what we could do in our heads as kids?' he asked.

Monica replied, 'Trouble is, inequality just leads to jealousy. Now life is only a privilege for the individually wealthy few, criminals and corporate interests.'

'Surely our success as a species has been built on our ability to co-operate to achieve our goals? We are told we live in an open, democratic society but the state always acts in the interests of capital.'

'It's all about negotiating boundaries. We live in the information civilisation now.'

'I just feel at this time, this push for consensus leaves me with the feeling of stagnation... What we need is a few more pop-up festivals, like the Edinburgh fringe, that kind of thing. I sympathise with those school kids on the streets.' Louise nodded. He continued, 'That's why I like the music here. Our way of life is under threat.

Clive said, 'There are two ways to change, one by solving the problem and one by ignoring it. Sometimes the only thing to do is walk away,' which is what he felt like doing.

Chapter 59

Clive was shocked. He had just put down the phone. His dad had heard on the TV of a drug bust in Muirside, with a large haul of skunk. The club had not been mentioned, but Beth had rung earlier with the clue. Clive had put two and two together. Was Pablo really involved? He had trusted him; the man had even bought him a few drinks and subbed him now and then. He had put together the open mike night in good faith. Louise had stayed the night at his flat after the gig from "Dubtown International". Apparently, there had been a tip-off (Russian Television) and it was all over the media now. Not good for the town at all, and worse still, and not for him either.

'I never really took to Judd, you know,' Louise sobbed. 'I thought he was just a gabby used-car trader, I hardly knew him. He seemed to have a wide circle of friends. Obviously, there was more going on.'

Clive nodded, 'Yes, there was, and Dad was puzzled and had his suspicions about what exactly brought him back up here, he was in bad company to be sure. I am no clairvoyant. Now I think, we knew.' He asked, 'What do we do now, then?'

'I must speak to Beth,' Louise dropped her mug. 'This feels like the strangest Sunday ever. Be honest with me, Clive, did you suspect this might happen?' He considered, 'Yes, I knew something was up. She had a tip-off from Martin, who used to clean there, she told me. You were never going to be in danger at the club. It was stick or twist.' He sighed, 'It will be the last gig we will ever see there, I believe.'

'And what has Monica got to do with that?'

'She gave me a card for an RT journalist and I am beginning to realise it was her who was tailing my stepbrother. Beth rang the number on the card. She is apparently going to meet Anya today or so she said.'

Chapter 60

Pablo yawned. It had been a really good gig. He made his way sleepily in to the kitchen and put the kettle on. Ramos and Juliana were safely over at his wife's flat. He turned the radio on. He needed to check his email.

'...Following a successful drugs bust on the Muirside estate, Dumfries police confirm they have arrested two suspects on suspicion of drug dealing at Bellingham Tower following a sting operation...' His heart lurched. They were ruined. It could be an arrest at any time if Judd talked.

He looked at his phone. He had a missed call last night. It was from Judd. It was another thread of evidence linking the two of them, though. Traceable records. Lots of them.

Pablo examined his options. He felt the sensation of despair. It had got to be Martin. Or could it be Anya? What had Judd said about her, muscling in on him in his flat with a sniffer dog; too late now to apportion blame. His head spun. He had never trusted that woman – all that stuff about meeting a friend?

A range of unpleasant choices beckoned; he was looking at a jail stretch, ruined reputation and possibly bankruptcy. His pride and joy would be sold off. His options were limited to run or destroy evidence. The more he thought, the better the first looked the best. The evidence was already up on the cloud. He had screwed up.

His club phone rang – the club landline. 'Omegaplex,' he said mechanically.

'Mr Perez, can you come down to the police station and answer a few questions?' The bell had toiled. Now he had to make the choice. He knew if he did not cooperate, they would come for him anyway.

'I can come in now.' He pressed the red button on the phone. He blinked. The blinds were shut, the TV silenced. He stared at the ceiling and shut his eyes again. He did not know whether he could take any more.

Chapter 61

Beth was puzzled. How come RT had already got hold of the story before she had even met Anya to tell her about it? She would give her a ring. It rang and rang. No answer. Something was wrong. It bugged her.

She frowned. She was tucking up her beloved Marilyn in her cot. Her mind turned to more pleasant memories. She was hoping to meet Clive in the next few days.

She would give Rochelle a bell and see if she had heard from her. She did not think she would now need to make a 3 pm rendezvous tomorrow. She sighed. What was going on?

Chapter 62

Rochelle fumed. She had received an upsetting phone call from Monica.

She was incandescent with rage, filled with righteous wrath. She had wanted to be treated as an adult and instead she had been duped as a child. She had never felt so betrayed or so angry. She was starting to hyper-ventilate, her chest was heaving.

A so-called journalist she had truly trusted; indeed someone she fancied; had turned out to be a complete fraud. Anya was a copper! She had heard it from Clive.

She slammed open her mobile and made her call. It was, to her surprise, answered straight away. 'You bitch! All smoke and mirrors with you, isn't it? Just doing your job, were you?'

On the other end of the line, Anya swallowed. 'Listen, Rochelle, the world is not as black and white as you would like to think. Yes, I had a job to do. And I have done it. We do have a drugs problem in this town, which you may or may not be aware of. Those drugs are causing addiction and that leads to crime. I do hope we can still remain friends. You have just strayed in this complicated situation. I know how hard this has been for you.'

Rochelle slammed the phone down. She was in bits. She had heard quite enough for one day. She never wanted to see Anya again. Another forgettable diary entry. She had been thrown underneath the bus.

Chapter 63

Rochelle sobbed into her phone. 'She's a cop, Beth. She never ever worked for RT.'

Beth was shocked. 'What?' She had always thought the woman was very glamorous for a journalist. She hadn't quite fit the bill, did she?

Beth did not know what to say. 'OK, let's meet up and have a chat.'

Rochelle asked, 'Where?'

'Let's meet at the usual, Beanz for Us, in an hour.'

Chapter 64

'Interview with Mr Pablo Perez, time is 10:16 am.' He was in the interview room at Frackburgh police station. 'Present Detective Inspector George Stanwell and Sergeant Peter Innes.

'You understand that you are being questioned in connection with an incident at Bellingham Tower last night involving drugs. You are being interviewed under caution.' He carried on, 'We believe you know what we are talking about?'

'I have no idea what you are talking about.'

'But you know Judd Laws, don't you?'

'Yes, he is a regular in the club. What has this got to do with me?'

'Come on, Mr Perez, he has told us everything. In your own time, please.'

'About what?' You never knew when there might be something worth taking in.

The Detective produced a bag of drugs. 'Does this look familiar?'

Pablo frowned. 'Is that what I think it is?'

'And what would that be, Mr Perez?'

'It does look dodgy,' he ventured. He didn't know what else to say. He felt hopeless, careless. He was definitely not at his best at such an improvisation. What could he say?

'We have now applied for a search warrant for your club and the associated flat.' Inspector Stanwell thought Perez was just playing along.

'I understand.' He swallowed, clenched his teeth. Had he just implicated himself? Was it time to pack his bag?

'You may go now. Interview terminated at 10:40 am.'
He was led out.

Chapter 65

Morton was talking to his friends, they were all off to an "Extinction Rebellion" march on a Friday when they would normally have been in college or school. It had all been organised on social media. They had all gathered in the bandstand of the local park, a diverse collection of human beings.

An older woman holding one end of a banner ("Capitalism isn't working") said that she was furious with Teresa May for saddling her children with debt and may well vote for the green party at the next election. Morton recognised Rob, the green box man.

He spotted Martin, who was a Facebook friend. He was talking to a guy he had once met, Angus was it? Somebody had even put on some grime on their music system. Angus had put his phone number in biro on his upper right arm, under his shirtsleeve, in case he was arrested.

A young man waving a red flag said, 'We're not in a revolutionary situation yet, but I think we might be soon.'

The thought that the streets of Frackburgh could be filled with street kids, disenfranchised youth, teachers, Barry the druid and old leftists, all united in the common cause was quite something. The eco-warriors had been there in the background all along, but now they had come out of the woodwork. Thrive within planetary limits, they said. Barry had spread out his hands to the sky. They were all the epitome of underdogs. Someone had even brought a ladder and was stencilling a mural on a hoarding. So much time and effort making protest seemed pointless, unpleasant and even dangerous.

Their form teacher had negotiated a route that Saturday that took them down the leisure zone of the town, Trylergate, towards the market square. The bemusement of onlookers was palpable. What did it take to raise an issue in this town compared to London? There was a massive stigma about being different. Would they be listened to or ridiculed?

But Mary with a "Wage Slave" label on rebuked Morton. 'I disagree that we're all talking about different things,' she said. 'The exclusion of women and their subordination to men; the kind of world we want to see is the same world – a world where money is used to help people. We're all just talking about different bits of it and saving the planet, not lobby groups who represent industry interests.'

Morton lay down in a doorway. He had taken a bit of cocaine last night and was now feeling woozy. He wanted his life to mean something, he knew he was stymied in his powerlessness. 'It's not what it looks like.' He was talking to Martin.

'Isn't it?' said Martin.

'How long before the medieval debtor's prison is reinstated? You want to carry on in this shithole?' asked Morton.

'I have a plan, involving the club. I want it burnt down,' said Martin.

'Let's speak to Angus, he could help.'

They ended up at Beanz for Us. It had been a good day. One that would have repercussions.

Chapter 66

Pablo had decided to do a runner. He would just disappear. His parting shot was to empty the till. You only live just the once, he reasoned. There had, however, been a firebomb attack at the rear of the premises, which he hadn't even noticed. At least he still had his grey felt hat.

Detective Stanwell had broken in, now that he had the search warrant to do so. He had spoken to Anya's handler in Dumfries, who was furious with him about the search warrant. Surprisingly, Pablo's computer was still there. He would have expected that to have been taken. He had a theory that he would be able to crack the password. But how long would that take and would there be anything on it of interest? He was organising a search of the premises for any clues.

They had not yet got any firm evidence to arrest him anyway. Judd had not said a word but he would go down anyway, caught red-handed as he was. For the police, it was nothing short of a disgrace, though, that the big fish might slip away, not uncommon in these cases. Where was the evidence? True they had a warrant for his arrest and his disappearance was timely. Where was he?

Chapter 67

Judd was in the police cell at Dumfries HQ. He was shivering with fear. Sweat was pouring down the inside of his shirt, his hair was damp. His counsel had just visited him.

If he snitched on Pablo, he had said, it would likely get his sentence reduced, apparently. He was looking at quite a few years behind bars anyway. He did not even know when the trial would be. He sank slowly down the walls, to sit on the floor of his cell. He was unaware that his main man had already flown the nest. If he had known that, he might well have taken up that offer.

How had he allowed himself to get mixed up in this? It was easy money, is all.

Chapter 68

Denise was livid. Pablo had simply disappeared after his interview with the police. There had also been an arson attack on the club. How was she supposed to support her kids? His phone was unobtainable. Apparently this guy Judd was at the police station HQ under lock and key. She had heard it all on the RT TV channel, which seemed to be well informed. She was shocked to her very core. She had suspected that something did not add up, but this! It was all too much. She shook her head.

The Police had "dismantled" her husband. How much more could she cope with?

Chapter 69

Anya had been called into Dumfries HQ. Her silver superior, Chief Inspector looked at her, hands propped to his chin. 'One out of two is better than, Anya.'

'We might find enough evidence in the club. Phone records, for example. I'm surprised he failed to burn the club down.'

Detective superintendent Piper continued, 'We can't be certain that was him.'

'Really? Who then? He can't run forever, can he?'

'Anya, time for your exit strategy. How does Stranraer sound?

'That will do nicely, sir. Distance is a great thing.' She paused, 'I do hope we have closed that club for good. We are the defenders of the realm.'

'Anya, know this, he didn't even have a PRS licence for his live music, we can take him to the high court if all else fails. I am sending you for psychological counselling tomorrow, by the way, so come in.'

Chapter 70

The computer was in the police lab. The techies were running a password-cracking programme. It had already tried two thousand combinations, without any success. Detective Stanwell asked, 'Can we try dates of birth, family names and so on? It might be the shortcut we need.'

'Well, not with this programme, we will have to do that manually,' he sighed. The tech was right. This was going nowhere fast. The trouble was, they had found no incriminating documents at the club. Not a single one. Of course, they could run through the accounts but it wasn't going to be there, was it? So all that they had left were mobile phone records and that was all they had. The old number was now unobtainable, surprise, surprise.

Regular contact between two people hardly constituted definitive evidence, but it was the best hope now. He hoped to God they had not used encryption, like Snapchat. One or better, several, incriminating conversations might be enough to convince a jury. He was on to it. Witness evidence would clinch it if Martin could be persuaded to testify. If they had used unregistered mobiles it was going to take time. If he could get Judd's number, it would be a start. He picked up the line for Dumfries. Pablo's wife would surely confirm the number she had for Pablo. He would ask her if she knew Judd's number.

Chapter 71

Pablo was in a call box somewhere out in the country with the jeep. Knowing the position of the cameras the police used, he had stuck to country roads, taking him away from the filling station camera. He was desperate to know where Judd was being held. Had he talked? Once he got to prison, he would be easier to get hold of, most likely in a police cell somewhere.

He had emptied the till at the club, but that was about all, apart from an overnight bag. He had not hung around in case the police came. Pablo was well aware he was now a running man in a marked jeep. He then realised he should have left with his laptop, but he had not been thinking straight. Still, it would take them time to crack his password.

He was ringing his wife, Denise. This was not going to be an easy conversation, but he had some responsibility for his family, however, estranged they might be.

He was through to her. He dropped the coins in the slot. 'Where are you, you bastard?'

He piped up, 'Listen, I'm calling from a callbox in the country. I have a confession to make.'

'Well, maybe you need to speak to a priest, not your wife. OK, what do you have to say to me?'

'I did something wrong, it was to support my family.'

'Don't drag me into this; I have to bring up your kids. How am I supposed to live? You really like pushing your luck, don't you?' She wanted to believe his recent actions had been a disastrous mistake but it was part of a continuing pattern.

He replied, 'Of course, I don't. It was simple expediency, yes?'

'Oh yeah, I can see why you are not using your mobile. The police have already asked me for Judd's number by the way,' she tittered.

His heart gave a lurch. They were after the phone records.

'Hand yourself in, Pablo. You have already sailed too close to the sun. You won't get very far with automatic number plate recognition, will you? Why did you set fire to the club, by the way?'

'What! No, not me!' *Had it been a rival dealer?* he wondered. *Did Judd perhaps have a rival who was on to him as well?* He piped up, 'Why would I set fire to my own club?'

Time for her to take charge. 'You tell me. Well, somebody has, no great damage if you want to know, just a bit of charred brickwork in the back alley.'

He was at a loss for words. 'OK, I will hand myself in.'

He got into his jeep and eased the vehicle back on to the road. It was over. He had to hand himself in.

Chapter 72

He presented himself to the custody sergeant. 'I believe you have been looking for me.' He had arrived at Frackburgh police station. The Sergeant looked up, frowning. 'Pablo Perez, Omegaplex.'

Understanding dawned. He was on the blower to Detective Stanwell. Upon receiving the call, Detective Stanwell asked his Sergeant to accompany him. That was the rule, always a second man present. 'I'm going to push him hard; I won't give him time to change his mind.' The other nodded. They needed to have a strategy.

Pablo was led to the same room as before. 'Interview with Pablo Perez. Present Detective Inspector George Stanwell and Sergeant Peter Innis. Time 3:30 pm. Mr Perez, you are under arrest for drug dealing. You do not have to say anything. But it may harm your defence if you do not mention when questioned something, which you later rely on in court. Anything you do or say may be given in evidence.'

'Can I have a solicitor?'

'In due course, Mr Perez.'

'How long have you been running this club, Mr Perez?

'Just over two years, officer.'

'How long have you been getting bands over from Jamaica?'

'I believe, about a year and a half.'

'We have been looking at your call logs.'

He groaned.

'It seems you have more than a passing acquaintance with Judd Laws; 499 calls in the last six months, in fact.'

'Some of these calls portend the exchange of items or as you call it the "drop". This seems to coincide with Saturdays. How can you explain that for us?'

Pablo gulped. He said, 'No comment.'

'We can draw our own conclusions, then, we will ask for bail to be refused.'

'Interview terminated at 3:45 pm.'

They led him away to the police cell. He had called his solicitor and he was due tomorrow. He put his head in his hands. He felt like a total idiot.

Chapter 73

Beth had arranged to meet Rochelle at Beanz for Us in the market place. The weather was glorious, but neither of them had noticed. 'Thanks for ringing, Beth.' Rochelle stared her in the eye. 'When were you ever a victim? Do you know what it feels like to be betrayed by somebody you loved?'

Beth re-joined, 'Of course I have been betrayed, from day one in the orphanage, by my real mum and by Anya. She lied to both of us. It was a mixture of truth and lies.' She added, 'You don't get to be a woman without seeing the uglier side of people.'

Rochelle took a long drag on her cigarette. She was close to tears. 'Did Clive say something about your upbringing?'

'Yes, it was touchy.' She paused. 'Look, Rochelle, you trusted someone, just don't try to turn it into a philosophical statement. All this talk about women being nurturing is just total crap. When the chips are down, we can be every bit as ruthless as men. Anya was acting the whole time, we both knew her. We just couldn't see it.'

'I don't know if it is worth carrying on.'

Beth banged the table, the coffee cups jumped. She was taken aback by Rochelle's resignation. 'Don't do a pity party on me, OK?' Customers at adjacent tables were looking at them, waiting to see if it posed any threat to their sense of harmony.

The manager had noticed, but was running a watching brief.

Beth looked her in the eye. 'Rochelle, get some perspective. Look at a really strong, genuine woman, look at Monica. She works in an all women charity, she doubled with me behind the bar, she organised a talk by a Buddhist monk!'

Rochelle replied, 'Yes, I suppose so.'

'And didn't you tell me Anya got you into work, yes?'

'Yes, true too.'

'Well then. I have to find another job, but I don't whine about it, do I? You have still had yours. You have free will; you don't have to become a big fat gypsy wedding. Cool your boots.'

Rochelle stood up. 'Thank you, Beth. You know this from experience.' They both hugged.

Chapter 74

Denise wept. This is just the beginning. How was she supposed to come to terms with her last conversation with Pablo? Nobody, surely, in the history of the universe, had to listen to such a pathetic, self-serving bunch of crap. OK, he was never a nine to five sort of guy, but this was a step too far! Surely he would hand himself in soon. Despicable man.

Ramos pulled a face at her. She did not care. How could she possibly explain that their father was a criminal? Not on. Juliana, by contrast, was oblivious.

She had to be back at work tomorrow evening and now needed a childminder. She was dialling the Samaritans. How was she going to get by? She also needed to ring Beth for her thoughts. It was all too much. She bottled her rising anger.

Chapter 75

'Your mental equilibrium goes, and yes, your mental health too.' Anya was describing her feelings to the psychological assessor at Dumfries HQ. 'I didn't realise how much I would miss the buzz, either, Lorna.'

She looked up at Anya. 'We needed to review your legend building anyway if you are to carry on. As you know, we do that every six months. What we now need to make sure is that you are ready to return to other policing duties. It takes some time to adjust, I agree.' Lorna knew she had to take down Anya's replies before her own memory had time to edit them. She took notes on her legal pad.

'As I said, I am concerned it may take you a while,' Lorna said. 'Yes, it was an acting role, but in normal acting, you stop being the actor when the play is over. What is absolutely essential is that you never come across any person you have befriended in the course of "Operation Priam". If you break this rule, that is what we term "going native".'

'Yes, I am aware of that.' Her eyes narrowed. 'It is all very well for you to tell me that. You have never had to go into that zone.'

'Fair enough, but you should be aware too that there is an ongoing public inquiry into undercover policing activities. This is a huge concern for our legitimacy. It also means that there may be anger towards you if you reveal your own role. I cannot say any more than that.'

Anya had burst into tears. She had betrayed her friends at the government's expense. She had come to love Rochelle. It was exactly the same trap that climate camp betrayer had fallen in to. Mark Kennedy was his supposed name.

Lorna told her, 'You need to see me at this time again in a week. I am not at all sure you are ready.' She held her hand in sympathy.

Chapter 76

Come the next day, rather than face up to reality, Anya had returned to the LGBT bar Reynards. She was most likely never to meet anybody she knew, except Jules. She needed space to think. Either that or she could have drawn a square on the floor and announced that it was her personal space. She was pretty sure Rochelle would never come here out of her own volition. She was feeling exactly what her psychologist had described to her – increasing irritation. She never expected this would happen. Not to her. But it had. Where was their personal duty of care for maintaining her mental wellbeing? The female sociality and solidarity that enabled women to stand up to men Rochelle wanted.

The truth was she enjoyed acting as the journalist. She had revelled in her role-play. She had no friends in Stranraer, which was where she would be posted. She either had to put this behind her or she could not carry on. Perhaps change her career altogether? It was tempting.

She felt safe here; maybe it was her only safe space now. She sipped her vodka and tonic. How long was she going to run? No RT, no daughter. An existence mediated by gaming and social media world more compelling than her reality.

She had not bothered to answer Beth's call, but she had recognised the number. She needed to getaway.

Chapter 77

Beth was returning a call from Denise. 'Denise, pull yourself together! I will not turn my back on you, understand?' She continued, 'I will babysit for you. The Samaritans can help with this kind of thing but you need to contact them. I am going to check out the daughter story myself.'

'Beth, you can't know how upset I am,' Denise sobbed. Her voice sounded lifeless and weak. 'Ramos and Juliana are acting up too. What am I supposed to tell them? They know something is wrong.'

'You are not the only one, I had a similar call from Rochelle, you know. You don't know her, I think, but she was also another friend duped by Anya. I can come around now for a cup of tea, if you want, Denise. Ring me anytime.'

Chapter 78

He put his briefcase on the table. 'Mr Perez.' He paused for effect, 'I need to know all the facts if you want me to defend you in court.' The solicitor spoke in a low and calm voice, 'You are looking at a custodial sentence I am afraid.'

Pablo looked into the eyes of the solicitor. 'I knew that.' They were in the interview room yet again at the police station. Pedro was handcuffed on one wrist to their table. Was this all life had left to offer?

'I will tell you whatever you need to know.'

'Have you given the police the password to your computer? Is there anything incriminating on it?'

'Not that they could find.' Pedro frowned. 'I used the darknet, I won't lie, and they won't trace that.'

'Have anything further to tell me? Anything further could be helpful.' He frowned. 'A bit of co-operation could help reduce your sentence, Mr Perez. You should look at that again. I also have to tell you that they are looking to shop you for lack of a public entertainment licence, a PRS. That would be a fine.'

Pablo groaned. He was going to be ruined. He had pawned his future.

Chapter 79

Clive furrowed his brow. He could no longer have his charity gig at the Omegaplex; he would have to find another venue in town. They would also need to find a band with a PA and drum kit.

He picked up his mobile. He would ring Monica. 'Mon, are you OK to talk? What I am thinking is maybe this is not the time to press ahead, without a venue.'

Monica replied, Clive, 'I think we should do it, at least give some support the music community who had invested so much effort in the Omegaplex. Yes, it has made the job riskier. I tell you what, let me track down a band with a PA, you find the venue.'

Clive beamed. 'Thanks, Monica, you are right as usual.' He picked up his list and proceeded to dial. Twenty-one bands to ring around. His list was ready. Rocktober it was! He had already felt under enough day-to-day pressure without this to deal with.

Chapter 80

Detective superintendent Piper was speaking to Chief Inspector Boyd at Dumfries HQ. He was debriefing Gold command for "Operation Priam", Chief Inspector Gordon. 'So this has been a success?'

Detective Superintendent Piper replied, 'Not entirely. I have passed the files to the Crown Prosecution Service. Luckily, Perez handed himself in, those idiots at Frackburgh should never have interviewed him under caution before applying for a search warrant. Whatever happened to deference, they said they had no choice! If it was not for his mobile records, we would have had nothing to go on. I have spoken to Detective Stanwell there and had words. I am afraid, sir, that this has raised jurisdiction issues between bronze and silver. I need to resolve this in future. Such a lapse in judgement will luckily never be made public.'

'Maybe. It is also conceivable that everything will eventually end up in a newspaper, what with the forthcoming enquiry into undercover policing. What about the undercover officer modifying her legend as a Russian mafia with the secondary runner Judd? You have done due diligence on that, I trust? Any suggestion that state entrapment did occur would result in a stay of proceedings.'

'No, that was within the law and even if he had taken the Russian-funding bait, it would have been. We only presented the defendant with an unexceptional opportunity to commit a crime. However, Anya took that new identity on the fly without my authorisation and has been reprimanded for it. I would never have sanctioned that. Her enthusiasm for her role has got out of hand.'

Silver continued, 'I am concerned, moreover, for her mental health and the psychotherapist is extremely concerned, she is keeping it under review. Our golden girl seems to have taken quite a hit from the whole operation. She can be a mischievous provocateur.'

'Go on,' Inspector Boyd had not interrupted.

'A further issue has arisen from an arson attack on the Omegaplex. Perez denies he did that.'

'Can he be trusted with anything? Could he just be lying?'

'I rather doubt it, he seemed genuinely surprised. There is no obvious motive for him to burn his own premises down. He has no incentive to lie, he is in deep already. If he is telling the truth, it suggests there could be a third-party actor still out there. That could mean a turf war. I have no leads on that at all, but I will ask our UCO, Anya. Understanding is not comprehension. Understanding is merely recognising it doesn't add up.'

'Does it really matter if the club has been closed?'

'Well, yes sir, it matters to me, I am concerned there may be a rival who can pick up the business. I will leave enquiries open when I write my final report.'

Chapter 81

'Anya, we need to wrap up a few loose ends. I believe you have an informer on the Muirside estate?' She was at the Dumfries HQ talking to Chief Inspector Piper.

'Oh, you mean Angus, the halfway house. Yes, I paid him for information. He does live in the same tower block as Jimmie, sir. I believe he has got into amateur dramatics, the Paladonian.'

'Is he on the straight and narrow? Anya, could he be our arsonist?' He put his elbows on the table, looking her in the eye. 'Has he returned to his criminal ways?'

'I suppose, it is possible. His sentence was theft not arson. Not that I have spoken to him recently. Sir, I have only met him twice.'

She frowned, 'He would have a motive, I suppose, if he were a dealer.'

'Anya, please make discreet enquiries. You don't have to move to Stranraer, you are under the psychologist. She is concerned about you.'

Anya said, 'I'm in no mood to quarrel, sir. I will think of a way.'

Chapter 82

Beth was checking out the Anya-daughter story. She had contacted St. Andrews University. Their website had already confirmed they did not have a music course. Her telephone call confirmed it was so. As she thought; it was another tissue of lies from Anya. What was unravelling here, she realised, was deception on a planned scale.

This was hard to comprehend and she had decided to contact the Guardian newspaper. They had been appealing for just such information ever since the infiltration of the climate camp and other pressure groups. It reminded her of the routine lies she had put up with at the orphanage. Memories that were painful and lasting.

Strike while the iron was hot. Clive had been round first thing on his way to work. She had filled him in. Maybe the reporter could put her mind at rest; they had been appealing for information on undercover ops, so Monica had been telling her.

Chapter 83

Clive was feeling out of sorts after work and not particularly hungry. He, at least, could look forward to an Italian at Giovanni's, one of the oldest restaurants in the town. Maybe this shindig with Judd had raised issues of his own. Work was not going well; if he did not take a day off soon, he was going to feel worse.

He stepped into the restaurant, walking straight out there from the office. It was only five minutes away. Beth had beaten him to it; she was already sitting at the bar. 'Hi.' Giovanni's had been set up after the war and was famous for its Italian pasta and pizza. He noticed her sleeveless halter neck top. She did look ravishing. She told him she had persuaded a distraught Denise to babysit, in return for her looking after Ramos and Juliana tomorrow, when she was on a hospital shift. He was taking a day off to do that.

The waiter was shouldering his way through the kitchen swing doors, laden with a tray of food. Clive spoke, 'We have reserved a table for two.'

The waiter put his napkin out over his arm, 'The name sir?' he asked.

'Welbeck,' replied Clive.

'Follow me,' and led them up to their table by the side window.

They sat down. The manager then came over to welcome them. 'My father was here as a prisoner of war, he stayed and started this place,' he explained. They nodded. 'Welcome.'

'Beth, thanks for joining me.' He looked into her eyes. They continued studying the menu. Her eyes met his.

'I wish I could believe in vegetarianism like that Buddhist was talking about,' he said, 'but I have tried it and I just don't get enough protein in it.'

'I agree. It is virtuous but you don't get by without supplements, particularly B12 and protein. Monica seems to manage it though.'

'Beth, nature can be cruel.'

The waiter had returned to their table. Were they ready to order? Did they want a starter?

'Yes, that would be nice. No need to be parsimonious. Say minestrone soup?' Beth nodded.

'OK.'

'And for the main course, Madam, Sir?'

'Well, Margherita pizza for me, what about you, Beth?'

'How about the lasagne?'

The waiter piped up, 'Our lasagne contains four layers of pasta, cheese and lamb mince.'

'Nice, I will go for that,' she said. She turned to her companion. 'Clive, I have lost one of my two jobs, while you still have yours,' she frowned.

'I have reached an impasse,' he sighed. 'Liberalism, what I embrace, isn't working, not at my workplace, anyway.'

'Why do you say that it sounds fatalistic?' she parried. She was reluctant to accept this, so she said, 'There's bound to be the odd personality clash in any organisation.'

He replied, 'I want to reach out. I have in mind non-exec director for Frackburgh Housing Action Trust. I spoke to an agency who is dealing with it.' He continued, 'I am also on the Green Party MEP shortlist.'

'Not sure about that. I do have some good news for you though,' she replied. 'Monica has got us a band with a PA!' she smiled. 'By the by, Clive, how are you doing with a new gig venue?'

'Nothing yet.' He looked in her eyes, 'I will keep trying for Monica.'

'What about me?' He had said the wrong thing. He paused with a slice of pizza in his mouth. 'No, for all of us.'

He paused, took another mouthful. 'Listen, this is the real, authentic me, not the fake one I pretend to be as an architect draughtsman.'

'Oh, not the pity party again.'

But Clive had not finished yet.

'I would love to be the person you want me to be. Yes, I am trying to balance my inclinations with my duty. All those bleak years I spent at architectural school, having the shit ripped out of me when I pinned up my work.'

Their starters had arrived. They tucked in. She waved her fork at him. 'We are supposed to be eating. I haven't mentioned my convent upbringing again, have I?' She paused. 'Perhaps there is something I could suggest, though.'

He was silent as he took another mouthful of food.

'OK, here is my idea, Clive. Are you listening? We form ideas co-operative, call it "B flat 5", whatever. It will be an act of solidarity. We use it to promote music, drama and film, whatever. No longer dependent on one dodgy club owner. We would be properly constituted, a charity or some co-op setup perhaps. Now Monica would be on board for that.'

Clive stared at her. 'Are you serious?' He continued, 'That would be brilliant.' He assented.

This was definitely the crux. He appreciated the strength of her idea. 'How is your lasagne?' he asked.

'Beautiful!' She did not want to admit this to herself, but she was falling in love with him. He could be hard work at times, but worth it in the long run.

'I tell you what I don't get. It is one of life's many mysteries. We have a well-paid service based economy, like cutting hair, painting nails, cutting grass and walking dogs. We do all these things and earn £26k and buy things from China where people toil in factories for a pittance to what we earn. I don't know how this works. You'd think the exchange rate would correct that – but the Chinese are pegged to the dollar.'

'Yes, it's a funny old world,' she replied. 'We seem to be doing all right.' She smiled.

Chapter 84

Something caught Anya's eye. She had decided on her dress-down hooded outfit for this visit, as she had the previous time she had called at Bellingham Tower. She hoped to meet Angus. A window was opened and the sun was glistening off a ground floor window in the flat occupied by Angus. So he was in at least. She was investigating the arson attack on the Omegaplex.

She had not rung him, an element of surprise would be important. How was she going to handle this? Probably with difficulty!

She started by "knocking" on the door and then buzzed the intercom.

BZZZ. 'Who is this?' the voice said.

'Anya from RT.'

'What do you want, woman?'

'Background research into the bust at the Omegaplex.'

'Come on in, if you must.'

He buzzed her in. She walked up to his front door. It opened. She registered the hostility in the young man's gaze. He was clenching his fist in his pocket. 'Supposing there is anything in it for me?' he sniggered.

'Look, I'm not trying to make friends. I am not trying to bust you for any old thing. You can be sure that you are helping the police and we are grateful for that.'

'How much?'

'Let's just talk, Angus. I can pay.'

'Bullshit!' The door was slammed in her face. She walked away. Her last assignment in town had ended. She would be off to Stranraer then.

Chapter 85

The window round the back of the Omegaplex was even smaller than it had looked from three metres below. The three of them hardly looked like a group whose role in life was to break the law, but in the wake of the recent abuse of power of undercover policing, they had all decided it was. It was coming up to sunrise and he needed to stay quiet until there was enough light. Clive anticipated that the alarm would not have been set because the police would not know the code.

Beth had identified the window to the female toilet as being a weak point. The latch to the female toilet window looked feeble, she had said.

'I will take your word for it,' said Clive. He hoped he could prise it open without having to break any glass.

OK, this was burglary, but the police had hardly shown the moral higher ground, had they? Beth, Clive and Monica all wore black tee shirts and jeans. 'Right, gloves on, everyone.' They were all in it now.

They had bought a ladder with them. They looked around to check the coast was clear. Clive started to climb. The window was levered, he turned on his torch and clambered through. It was a short drop to floor level; the others followed. The alarm had not gone off.

He pulled the lobby door, they were in!

Chapter 86

Of course it made perfect sense. 'He just clammed up on me, sir. If silence indicates guilt, Angus is our man.' Anya was at Dumfries HQ.

'Yes, I see your point, Anya. It can't be helped. But you have warned him off, we are on the case, now he knows. I very much doubt we can prove anything.' He continued, 'History does have a habit of repeating itself. He is under licence and he can still be back behind bars again.' He looked into her eyes. 'Anya, I have warned you before about going off-legend. Your RT tip-off could still backfire,' he sighed. 'I think you need to take a break before you are reassigned, Anya. Take a week off and get away somewhere, it will do you good. You can take Igor with you.'

'Thank you, sir.' It had been a mistake that would haunt her. She went out to her car to re-join Igor. She fancied a week at the seaside.

Chapter 87

'I want you to check out the Omegaplex again, Stanwell. We need more evidence on Perez for the drug dealing. Maybe he has written down some information somewhere and hidden it under a floorboard, wherever.'

His computer password was unhelpful in the event, even when Perez volunteered it because his emails were all encrypted on the dark web. Use of the dark web was inconclusive, in a case that demanded conclusive evidence. 'We at least have a front door key.' He added, somewhat unnecessarily, 'Let me know the moment you find anything.'

'Yes, boss.' What Detective superintendent Piper asked for, he would do. The piper calls the tune! He set off on his allotted task. He would have to rope in the fingerprint team.

'Free tomorrow? Right, we go in first thing. Dust a club.' He raised his eyebrows.

Chapter 88

The Guardian journalist had come up from London and she had met him at the railway station. Beth had taken him to Beanz for Us, as the weather was fine. She had Marilyn with her in the pram. She was fast asleep.

'Thank you again, Mr Probert, for coming to Frackburgh. We have been subjected to a covert police operation here, which has closed our best music venue in town.'

He asked, 'How long has this been unfolding?'

She thought, 'Well, pretty much three months, I guess.'

'How did it start?'

'Well, this supposed RT journalist started coming in on a Saturday I suppose about the same time as Judd did. I work, I mean worked, behind the bar at the Omegaplex on Saturday nights. I never suspected a thing until the drugs raid, when it all fell into perspective. It is really Martin, the cleaner, who was the trigger for that,' she narrated carefully with all the details.

She sipped her latte. He was thinking. 'We are at the start of an inquiry in public and this would be valuable background,' he said.

'Oh, I doubt Martin would want to give evidence. Pablo must have intimidated him, I believe.'

'Isn't he due to stand trial and be locked away?'

'Yes, but who knows whether there will be a successful conviction or when that will be? Only the police would know that.'

'Judd Laws is charged, though, isn't he, and Martin could submit an anonymous statement to the inquiry?'

'Yes, Judd will go down because he was caught red-handed. No date on his trial either. Monica, my friend behind the bar, will confirm the details I cannot remember.' She continued, 'There was a bit of odd behaviour one night when she challenged Anya for her RT card. When she left we had an underage drinking swoop. I put it down to coincidence, at the time. There was also a supposed daughter studying music at St Andrews. I have found that to be a lie, no such course exists.'

Malcolm Probert was scribbling on his pad. 'Would she speak to me, do you think?'

She turned towards him. 'I am sure she would. I can give her a ring.' She got out her mobile. 'She is a journalist herself, works for a local magazine.' She dialled the number.

'Mon, it's Beth. Sorry to ring you at work. You can talk? Good. It won't take long. I've got a journalist from the Guardian with me.'

Monica said, 'Are you for real, Beth?'

'Yes, he has come up from their London office. Can you slip out of your office at lunchtime and meet us at Beanz for Us?'

'Affirmative.'

She gave a thumbs-up to Malcolm.

Malcolm nodded. It was already half-past twelve. 'Shall I order something to eat while we wait?'

'Yes, I will need to do a nappy change soon anyway.' Boy, what a day!

Back at her office, Monica scratched her head. Beth had not mentioned she was thinking of this. It must be about the undercover operation. Would it affect her role at Namastaia? It had better not. It was her only source of income, since the demise of the Omegaplex. She had signed up for bar work at Wetherspoons, not confirmed as yet.

It was 1 pm. She put her coat on and walked down to the square. There was Beth with the journalist. Marilyn was shouting her head off, ready for a nappy change no doubt. Their eyes met. 'Let me introduce you to Malcolm Probert.

He has come all the way from London. Now, I have a nappy to change.'

Monica sat down.

'Would you like a coffee?' he asked.

'Love one, yes, please. I need to get some lunch too.'

'That's all on me, tell me what you want,' he beamed. He scribbled it down in his notepad and went inside to place the order.

Beth was coming back from the toilets with a contented baby. She went back into the pram and adjusted the pram.

'Now let's see how we are going to play this, Mon.'

'Beth, slow down!' she frowned as she sat down. 'Are you planning national press coverage?'

'Not necessarily, I told the Guardian about Anya's non-existent daughter at St Andrews. He needs to research what rules these people are supposed to be following.'

Then Malcolm re-appeared with a tray, laden with goodies.

'Let me introduce myself,' he now addressed Monica. 'Beth has asked me to come up here and research the pattern of events that have taken place around the Omegaplex. Malcolm Probert.' He extended his hand to shake.

He continued, 'As you know, authoritarian, totalitarian states, insecure in their power, have always fought privacy with their extensive networks of secret police, as have democratic countries, in times of unrest. Beth has filled me in on the details. It seems this has now been taken to the next level. You have followed my column in the Guardian?'

They both nodded their heads. It was going to be all right.

'We all want full disclosure,' Monica said. Malcolm Probert nodded.

Chapter 89

Detective Stanwell opened the front door of the Omegaplex. A stuffy, musty smell greeted him. Where should he start looking? He thought he would do a look around. He started in the basement and walked on to the stage area. Then he noticed something unusual. Was there not something missing? There was a hole in the woodwork where the mixing desk had once been, wires and plugs lying on the floor. What the hell?

He scratched his head. If you were Pedro, where would you hide a password or a USB stick even? Perhaps hidden on the underside of a desk or under some loose floorboard? The previous search had been fairly thorough, but not taking everything apart. This one would be more like looking for a needle in a haystack. Maybe there was more point in stripping his jeep?

He went to the male toilet, behind the stage. There was a cleaner's cupboard. He was sure that had been searched. The cisterns all had angled shelves over. Perhaps if he looked upstairs in the office? He took up the carpet, checking for loose floorboards. No, all fully nailed down, a big fat zero. Would it be the underside of the desk? He ran his hand under the edge of the worktop and bingo! There was something taped down there. He peeled it off. It was the address and phone number for a B and B. In nearby Newcastleton! What was the significance of that?

He picked up his mobile. He rung Dumfries police station. 'Detective Superintendent Piper, please.' It was picked up. 'Detective Stanwell here, sir. I have news from the Omegaplex. I have found a hidden business card for a B and B in Newcastleton. Let me give you the details. Oh, and by the way, there has been a break-in. It looks as if the mixing desk has been stolen, a rear window has been forced open.'

There was a pause before the super replied, 'I don't suppose anyone saw them? Well, make the usual enquiries, I will deal with the B and B.'

The detective grinned. *Probably not,* he thought. 'Yes, sir.'

Chapter 90

Malcolm Probert spread his hands out, palm down, flat on the table. 'This is what I can do for you.' It was lunchtime at Beanz for Us, talking to Beth and Monica. They had all finished eating. The sun was weak and there was a light breeze. 'We can keep this under wraps for now as it may be sub judice.' He paused. 'What I mean is, it may come up at trial, well, perhaps two trials, depends how the CPS decide to play it.' He waved a pamphlet in the air. 'Now, this is the manual for undercover policing, published by their training college of policing in Rugby. Have a read through it and see whether they have followed the rules. It will be crucial in court.'

'OK,' said Beth. Monica nodded. Admittedly, she could feel no great sympathy for Pablo, but at least they would get to the bottom of the police infiltration exercise.

They shook hands on that and he said he would find his own way back to the train station. 'Keep in touch,' he said.

An alliance had been forged. It would have inspired a different conclusion if they had not taken action. That would have been cowardice.

Chapter 91

The police car arrived outside Raymonde's guesthouse in Newcastleton. Detective superintendent Piper himself, a detective and a sergeant for added intimidation. They rang the bell. 'I have been expecting you, gentlemen. Please come in.' They took their seats in his office. 'Raymonde Ronaldo at your service.'

'Raymonde, do you know a Mr Pablo Perez of the Omegaplex club in Carlisle?'

'Oh, yes indeed. He is a very good client of mine. He brings over bands from Jamaica to play at his club and they generally stay here after their gigs at the club, over a weekend usually. I give him a favourable rate as he uses me thirty or more times a year.'

Inspector Piper frowned. 'I believe your establishment has come up several times on his phone record.'

Ray frowned. 'Is there a problem, inspector?'

Yes, there may be. You see Mr Perez is under arrest for drug dealing and it is suspected the drugs are coming over from Jamaica.'

'What!' Ron was now on his feet. 'I had no idea.' He sat down again.

'We are trying to ascertain the drug supply route and we need to eliminate his contacts from our enquiries. Let me be candid, how well do you know these people?'

'Not at all,' he recollected. 'We made small talk, is all.' He thought further. 'Some of them were here the previous year, so I might know the odd name, but no, nothing more, you know.'

The inspector leant over the table. 'Accepting that to be true, then you won't object if we apply for a search warrant, will you?'

'I have nothing to hide, I can assure you, inspector. Whether my guests will be happy about that is another matter.' He paused. 'It would really help me greatly if you could conduct it during the middle of the day when most will be out about their businesses.'

The inspector considered this. 'That seems reasonable. I will be in touch when I have the warrant.'

Chapter 92

Detective Stanwell was back at the Omegaplex. He was looking for fingerprints following the burglary. Was it the same people as the arsonist? He had no idea, no information. There were thousands of prints here and the thieves probably had gloves on anyway. Maybe one or two of them might be on their records, but anyway you looked at this, it was a colossal waste of time.

He was not even certain where they had broken in. True, the female toilet window latch was broken but even so, it was a good few metres above ground level. He could only shake his head. A lamp was flickering in the ceiling. He didn't know what it meant or how he should respond.

Whatever the inspector said he had to do. He was in the doghouse. He sat back in the chair with his arms clasped together behind his head, while his technician dusted for prints.

Chapter 93

A search warrant for Raymonde's guesthouse in Newcastleton had been issued. The police had agreed to leave it until 11 am on Monday morning. The fingerprint team accompanied Detective Stanwell, who had been called in by Detective superintendent Piper. The piper!

'This could take the rest of the day. Eight guest rooms, the common areas, toilets, the kitchen and Raymonde's own suite. They would start with that last one first, leaving guests more likely to vacate their rooms before the search.'

Stanwell thought it unlikely they would find anything. At least, they could eliminate this place from their enquiries. He sighed. Why did he always draw the short straw? One or two guests still in the lounge frowned at them but carried on reading their newspapers. They found nothing, nothing at all. Perhaps if he had gone in without prior notice? No, the horse had long since bolted. He had drawn a blank.

Chapter 94

It was the first meeting for their new venture, "B flat 5". Monica clasped her hands together at the table. Just the three of them for now; she sat facing Clive with Beth at his side. They were at Monica's flat on Trylergate, above the Flying Scot pub. The illicit burglary had cemented the partnership. It was their dark little secret.

'Let's talk about the level of organisation, the skills and resources required. Let's start with incorporation.' Monica was chairing the meeting. 'If we become a registered charity, we have to renounce politics. Whereas, if we become a company limited by guarantee, we are free to pursue named aims. That also limits our liability to £1. We need to make an annual accounts return is all, it is also future proof. We cannot be made personally liable for its unpaid debts.'

Clive nodded. 'That makes sense, I agree. Beth, what do you think?'

'I don't mind either way, to be honest. How much is all this going to cost, though?'

'About £60, mainly registration fees. Are we going to use "B flat 5"?'

'I have checked, that name is definitely available.'

'How can we go on from here? I'm still an optimist and a fighter, but we need to own something we can call our own,' replied Clive. 'Something we can be proud of.'

Chapter 95

Charity gig time. Halloween had finally arrived. Charity had indeed paid off, with "B flat 5's" regular gig at the care home deemed a success. Clive had found tonight's venue, the Guitar Works.

Beth had found a new band to do their dress rehearsal for an upcoming gig in Newcastle. They had already promoted the gig on Skiddle and brought a brand new Celestion PA, along with £20,000 worth of kit. The Vorchellos had graciously allowed their drum-kit and PA to be shared among the six bands tonight with the 5 kilowatts PA. So they had kept shtum about their ownership of a mixing desk from the old Omegaplex. Everybody had a 20-minute set, with a changeover of 10 minutes between sets. The calibre of these acts was impressive. Friends and family were in the audience. Monica ran the raffle, prizes donated by the print shop.

Clive would be on the door all night; it would be a test of teamwork for the soon-to-be "B flat 5". Rock against Racism was a front for NASUWT, a teacher's union. It was taken for granted that it would be supported in an age of multiculturalism.

'Did you doubt yourself, just for a moment?' Monica was talking to Clive. There was only room on stage for a four-piece band and they had to split takings with the venue, but it was all in hand. There was no parallel to what they had achieved tonight. It was going to raise the money.

Chapter 96

Clive was back in the office. He was mulling over a call from Monica about her younger brother Morton. He had to decide whether he wanted to get involved in this family dispute. Worst of all it concerned the former Omegaplex. Oh what to do?

He would sleep on it and come up with a decision, he decided.

It was back to the job. The boss was unhappy about progress on the hostel extension. So was he!

Chapter 97

Rochelle had continued at the Letisea call centre on Frackburgh business park. It was tedious for sure but gave her some independence. She was still smarting from her futile encounter with Karen, a vendetta that seemed destined to continue. She still missed Anya but whenever she thought about her, she became angry.

She felt the pioneer in her family, vilified for having a job outside the traveller community. Something that to be held against her, apparently. Her dad's family business – horse-trading – could have grown over time with the right people, but Father wasn't actually that interested in engaging with the real world.

She put her hands behind her neck. She had to reclaim her own dignity.

Chapter 98

Anya was leaving the railway station. She was setting off to Blackpool for a week to get away from her undercover blues. She hoped she would not be recognised on the concourse. She was fairly sure nobody had followed her, but she needed to be wary. With her was her faithful hound, Igor, who seemed uncertain about what was going on. Not the only one, she thought. They would be happier on the Blackpool promenade, she hoped.

The train drew in, she got on, found her seat, reserved on the window side. Igor looked at her. He could not understand this car, it was enormous! He eventually settled under the luggage rack. She had bought a dog bowl and filled it up with water for him. He worshipped Anya.

Do we create our own reality? she wondered. She could only hope that she would be in a better frame of mind after this break. The worst thing was that she could never talk to her family about all this.

Chapter 99

Nina was dishing up at the Rolanda Care Home. The residents had started to arrive for breakfast, mostly by zimmer frame. Monica's grandma lived here. She was descendant from the Windrush generation.

All morning, she had plenty to do. Care workers were the backstop for the elderly. Getting the old dears up and changed. She needed more sheets and went into the store. Shelves were filled with boxes of medical gloves, tissues, syringes and colostomy bags, together with the linen store. Always busy in a care home.

She was training up the newbies, the new annual intake of recruits who joined every autumn. For this, she was paid the pittance of ten pence an hour extra. The shifts were long, 12-hour days, 12-hour nights.

"B flat 5" had agreed to provide residents' entertainment. Monica's grandma was a resident here. This would be their first co-operative venture, the one they had evolved to create. Now there were no regular gigs for Saturdays, they had time to do this.

'Nina, is my grandson coming to see me today?'

Mavis was eating her lunch. The room was festooned with Shamrocks as well as zimmer frames. Eileen King was playing at the music centre.

'Yes, he is coming over with your niece, after tea. They are going to play some music for you. We hope to make it a regular gig.'

They had arrived. They would be using the mixing desk today. Clive had been pretty sure nobody here would recognise it as an Omegaplex item.

'That would be nice,' said Mavis. 'It is great to see my daughter organise entertainment this evening.' She paused to think. 'I'm lucky to live here compared with my mother, you know.'

'Oh, and why would that be Nina?'

'She was locked up at my age in Lauder House, gone a bit senile you know.'

'That's terrible, Mavis.' She was shocked. 'To treat people with dementia by locking them away in an asylum.'

She moved on to another room. Flo was trembling, not good. She pressed the panic button. It looked like a seizure. The staff nurse came in, they exchanged looks. 'I'm calling 999, she said. Stay with her.' When the ambulance arrived, they bundled her away on a flatbed trolley.

'Go with them.' The paramedics were talking to Flo. They had wired her up. 'Looks like arterial defibrillation, doesn't it?'

Nina asked, 'Is she going to be all right?'

'Yes, we are giving her a shot to stabilise her.'

They drew into the A&E at Frackburgh General.

Chapter 100

Clive bundled Monica into his car. He had spent a night of broken dreams trying to come to a decision. They set off, hot foot to the shared house where Morton had locked himself in his flat. Not before ringing Monica, his sister, the day before. Clive was supposed to be at work but he had phoned in sick.

Morton had told her he was involved with the attempted arson at the Omegaplex. They had never had any secrets. This was an extremely worrying and most unwelcome development and she wanted to have a talk, she had told him she would be there in 15 minutes.

They arrived outside with a screech of brakes. And both leapt out, slamming the doors shut. They rang the bell but there was no response. They tried the door, she picked up her mobile and dialled. No answer. She shouted through the letterbox.

Morton had decided to jam the lock so nobody could come in. He slipped some paperclips into the tumblers. It was the mortice lock to the front door. He had behaved really stupidly but he blamed Angus, who had got him into cocaine.

'Morton, I know you are in there! Let me in. I need to talk to you.'

'OK, OK.' He was being an asshole. He took the clips out of the door and opened it using his key.

'Come in.'

Monica introduced Clive. 'We came here as soon as we could.'

'Sorry, sis, I'm not thinking straight.' He shook his head. 'I got friendly with Martin, who used to work at your club. I met him and a guy called Angus, at the Extinction Rebellion march. It was Martin who suggested the petrol bomb attack. I can't think why I got involved. I am trying to apologise.'

'Why, Morton?' Monica was exasperated with her brother. 'Look at yourself in a mirror. You know that club meant a great deal to me!

'Yes, I know all. Martin – I used to work with him, he has a grudge.'

'There's nothing as cleansing in the world as a good fire.'

She shivered. 'Who is this Angus guy anyway?'

'He lives in Muirside.'

'OK.' That place filled her with a sense of dread.

Chapter 101

Monica had spotted Anya at Frackburgh railway station, where she had gone to meet a friend. Anya appeared to be returning from afar, laden with a trolley and following dog. Monica glanced at her. Anya saw her approach. She froze. She had been warned what could happen.

It struck her as quite likely the end of her police career. She had always realised that a real journalist was most likely to unmask her. Was it time to "go native"?

Monica stabbed a finger at her. Anya hoped she was not going to lunge at her. She threw caution to the wind. 'I know what you are going to say, I have already decided to leave the police, Monica.'

'Really?' She really had not expected that! 'You should become an actress, is what I think. What are you purporting to be today?' Monica tittered. 'Where is your daughter?'

Anya squirmed. 'Forget it.' This was a face-off.

'Honestly, Anya, I don't really care much what you want to do. You have only just arrived, but hear this. You should know that I have passed what I have discovered to the Guardian newspaper.' She raised her voice. 'Just stay away, do you hear? And leave Rochelle alone.'

Anya stone-walled.

'My brother Morton knew Martin, they were involved in setting fire to the Omegaplex, encouraged by a lowlife called Angus. Bet you don't know that.'

Now that did catch her attention. 'Did you say Angus?'

'I did.'

She re-joined, 'I do know who you mean but I am grateful for that information.' With that, she walked off with her trolley, a swift exit, followed by Igor the husky.

Monica frowned, so she knew this Angus, this surveillance society was everywhere! It was a mean thing, true, to shop her own brother, but he needed pulling up now. Something that was beyond her own ability, apparently.

Chapter 102

Anya was on the phone to Dumfries police HQ.

'Sir, Angus is our man.'

'Definite proof?' the Piper was surprised.

'I have just bumped into Monica. Unfortunate, I know, I was coming back from Blackpool. Unforgivable, but for what she told me.'

Superintendent Detective Piper was getting angry. 'You could jeopardise our entire prosecution case for the Omegaplex!'

'Hear me out, sir. She named Angus as the arsonist. Put up to it by none other than Martin the ex-cleaner.'

'Can that hold up in a court of law? I doubt it. Just hearsay.'

She said nothing. She was so burnt from this last experience, it was the end. 'Sir, I need to see the psychologist straightaway.'

'Yes, I think you do. I will ring you back.'

Chapter 103

Anya was speaking to her psychologist, Lorna. 'It wasn't my fault. It was a chance encounter, at the railway station. I was coming back from my leave. Monica despises me,' she sobbed. 'Then she threw a curve-ball at me, naming her own brother as implicated in a crime of arson.' She burst into tears again.

Lorna replied, 'I am going to sign you off for another week, Anya. You need to talk this through with me as much as you can when you are ready.'

'I agree. These are still my friends.'

'I warned you about "going rogue". A clean break would have worked.'

'It was good while it lasted. It was power without responsibility, I realise.'

Lorna shook her head. There was a lot of work to be done here. 'Come and see me again in the middle of the week, say Wednesday?' She leafed through her diary. 'Can you make 10:30 am?'

Anya nodded. She would be off to Stranraer next week to find somewhere to live. Her life in Frackburgh was over.

Chapter 104

The police were already on their way to Angus's gaff in Bellingham Tower. Detective Superintendent Piper relished the opportunity to nab the arsonist. Because he was released under licence, the standard of proof for Angus was lower. He would be interviewed under caution, as would Martin and Morton. Maybe somebody would lie and then they could proceed.

What was of more concern to him was whether a jury would convict Pablo Perez, once the full details of the infiltration became public, which thanks to Anya's big mouth, they now had. Martin was not going to be a witness, after all, unless he did a deal to forget the arson.

He picked up his mobile and dialled Inspector Piper. 'Sir, we have a messy situation here. On the Omegaplex case, Judd will go down, Perez could fail. Our potential witness, Martin, is now implicated in the arson attack.'

'Has he been interviewed?'

'Not yet. We have concentrated on Angus because we can put him straight back inside. The juvenile Morton will be charged and no doubt sent to a young offenders' institution. What am I going to do about Martin?'

'Offer him an ultimatum. If he does not appear as a witness in the Perez trial, we will pursue the arson charge.'

Detective Stanwell demurred, 'Have we actually got any concrete evidence for the arson?'

'No, but he does not know that.'

'Sir, I am not at all sure the Crown Prosecution service would allow that. Why not just do a civilian prosecution for lack of a public entertainment licence?'

'Let's wait and see. Have you redeployed Anya, the UCO?'

'Yes, she is now based in Stranraer.'

Chapter 105

Beth was talking to Monica. 'We should buy Omegaplex, Monica.'

'What!'

'Yes, it's up for sale.'

'How could we possibly afford that?'

'Clive wants to get a mortgage. He has been feeling restless for a while.'

'Blimey! You have surprised me, Beth.'

'He says he is getting a legacy from a relative.'

'I see.' She thought. 'Would it be a "B flat 5" venture?'

'He says that's the idea.'

Chapter 106

It was a late autumn afternoon. Angus was in the police station in Frackburgh. 'Interview with Angus Daly, time is 2:15 pm. You are being interviewed under caution. You do not have to say anything. But it may harm your defence if you do not mention when questioned something, which you later rely on in court. Anything you do or say may be given in evidence.'

Angus shifted uncomfortably in his chair. 'Listen, I was told by that Anya woman that she wasn't trying to stop me for anything. I done my time you know.'

'Well, what do you think we are going to ask you about?'

'No idea.'

'Arson.'

'You can't be serious. Can I have a solicitor?'

'It's only an interview. Do you know anyone called Martin?'

'Martin who?'

'What about a kid called Morton?' He was met with a blank stare.

'Who?'

Stanwell frowned. His entire theory was based on nothing more than intuition. Maybe Martin would be more talkative.

'No further questions.' Maybe he needed to go on a course to learn how to do this.

'Interview terminated at 2:45 pm. You are free to go.'

Chapter 107

Clive was thinking. He knew he had done it once, therefore he could do it again. He now had unexpected funds to buy the pesky Omegaplex. He would put up a sign, he thought, "under new management". It would be unlike anything he had done before.

Chapter 108

Morton had been called into the police station in Frackburgh. 'Interview with Martin Jarvis, time is 9:15 am. You are being interviewed under caution. You do not have to say anything. But it may harm your defence if you do not mention when questioned something, which you later rely on in court. Anything you do or say may be given in evidence. Do you understand?'

He had a social worker with him as he was still a minor. 'I do,' said Morton.

'Are you sure, Morton?' she said. What should she be expected to do about that?

'I know what we have done.' He put his head in his hands. 'I should never have done that.'

The detective was straight on the case. 'So tell us Morton, who actually set fire to the club?' He paused. 'You and who else, Morton?'

He had clammed up. 'No comment.'

'Does the name Angus mean anything to you?'

Morton scowled.

'It was Martin, cleaner from the club, who suggested it.'

'You do realise you have put yourself in a very difficult position?'

'Indeed.' Morton paused. 'It was my sister who reminded me of that. I am not proud of where I am. I just wanted a statement of identity.'

'You have been led astray, my son.' Detective Inspector Stanwell felt sympathetic. His own son was a hard case to handle. 'Are you willing to testify against Martin?'

'No, never.'

'That's not what I wanted to hear because you will become a borstal boy.'

Morton scowled. 'I always hoped for better but I did not have any faith.'

Chapter 109

Monica left her flat. She had just spoken to Morton's social worker. It did not bode well. She pushed her pram up the street. What would Mavis say? She was off to Rolanda care home to find out. She arrived at the care home talking to her mum, Mavis. 'Mum, brace yourself, we need to have a chat about Morton.' She put on her sternest look. 'Mum, sit down.' Mavis looked concerned.

'You told you he had fallen into bad company. Well, it has now gotten serious, but not even I expected him to tell me what I found out yesterday. I hoped his extinction rebellion march would have set him on the right path.' She frowned.

Mavis pulled a face. 'Monica, what has he done?' Consternation spread across her face.

'Attempted arson.' She hesitated. 'He is friendly with a drug dealer called Angus. They did a petrol bomb attack, apparently, he was in competition with another dealer called Jimmie Armstrong. My own brother!' Monica wept. 'He had such potential.'

Mavis did not know what to think. 'Have the police gotten involved, he is only 17?'

'They may put him in a youth detention centre.'

'Hmmm. That might do him some good, I think, he used to be a good boy,' replied Mavis.

'I agree,' she replied. 'We all hope he will learn.'